CONTENTS

Chapter 1	2
Chapter 2	5
Chapter 3	9
Chapter 4	12
Chapter 5	18
Chapter 6	26
Chapter 7	38
Chapter 8	43
CHAPTER 9	49
Chapter 10	53
Chapter 11	57
Chapter 12	60
Chapter 13	64
Chapter 14	67
Chapter 15	73
Chapter 16	77
Chapter 17	82

Chapter 18	86
Chapter 19	87
Chapter 20	92
Chapter 21	97
Chapter 22	102
Chapter 23	107
Chapter 24	113
Chapter 25	118
Chapter 26	124
Chapter 27	134
Chapter 28	146
Chapter 29	148
Chapter 30	152
Chapter 31	159
Chapter 32	162
Chapter 33	177
Chapter 34	181
Chapter 35	189
Chapter 36	194
Chapter 37	197
Chapter 38	206
Chapter 39	211
Chapter 40	217
Chapter 41	223

Chapter 42	232
Chapter 43	237
Chapter 44	241
Chapter 45	248
Chapter 46	251
Chapter 47	254
Books In This Series	258

The Bloodborn Project
Book 1 – Wolf Man

There are nights when the wolves are silent and only the moon howls.
George Carlin

CHAPTER 1

The room was dark. Vertical blinds covered the single window, blocking out the sun. A large desk stood in the middle. Behind it, a well-worn leather chair. In front, two more chairs, newer but of vastly inferior quality. Government Issue. The desk itself was old. Not antique, simply old. Shabby. But like the leather chair, it was solidly built. Quality workmanship.

A man sat in the comfortable old leather chair. He had silver hair, cut in military fashion, albeit slightly longer than regulation. He looked to be in his late fifties but well maintained. Too well maintained. A slight tension in the skin around the eyes. The flesh on his face a little too thin. Lips taught, too tight to fully relax. Burt Reynolds on a good day.

There was a knock on the door and the man in the leather chair pushed a button on the underside of his desk.

The door buzzed open.

Another man walked in. Dressed in a black suit, black shirt, black boots. On his hands, black gloves crafted from the finest kidskin, almost as thin as latex. A black Trilby hat. Aviator sunglasses. Around his neck, a black silk neckerchief. Skin as pale as a shroud.

He strode across the room, his movement beyond graceful. Liquid smooth. His footsteps soundless on the cheap nylon carpeting. He sat down on one of the inferior chairs.

'He's been spotted out East,' he said. 'Kentucky.'

'Are you sure?' Asked the man with the silver hair.

The man in black shrugged. 'It's never a one hundred percent thing when it comes to him. You know that.'

The man with the silver hair stood up and walked towards the window. 'How long have you been searching for him, sergeant Hopewell?'

'How long have *we* been searching, colonel?' Countered Hopewell. 'After all, I'm not the only one involved.'

'Point taken, sergeant,' conceded the colonel. 'Okay, how long have *we* been searching for him?'

'Just over fifty five years, sir.'

'Not that impressive a record, is it?'

'No sir,' agreed Hopewell. 'But I have brought many others to you. It's just that he is different. Special.'

The colonel nodded. 'Yes, Hopewell, you have returned many lost sheep to the flock. But we have no real need for sheep. What we want is the wolf.'

'I will find him, sir.'

The colonel reached out and twisted the rod that operated the blinds, opening them slightly to let in a shaft of sunlight.

The man in black hissed and pulled back. 'Please, sir.'

'Oh, of course,' said the colonel. 'I'm sorry. I forgot.' He closed the blinds with another twist of his wrist.

Sergeant Hopewell relaxed. He said nothing. He knew that the colonel had not forgotten. It was a warning. Subtle, but still there. Remember who you are, he was saying. Remember who holds the ultimate power in this relationship.

'When will you leave?' Asked the colonel.

'Tonight, sir,' answered Hopewell. 'As soon as the sun goes down.'

'Find him,' said the colonel. 'Find him and bring him back to me.'

The man in black nodded, stood up and left the room, closing the door behind him.

The colonel, twisted the blinds fully open, letting the sunlight flood the room. Then he sat down again, opened his desk drawer, took out a small bottle of hand sanitizer and disinfected his hands, distributing the gel in a slow and methodical fashion.

He did it twice.

But, as always, it made no difference. There was no way to wash out the darkness.

No way at all.

CHAPTER 2

U.S. Route 50 stretches from Sacramento, California, in the west, to Ocean City, Maryland, on the east coast. The Highway is marketed as "**The Loneliest Road in America**", a phrase originally derived from a very negative piece in Life magazine around 1987. In the article, they urged travelers to stay away from the emptiness of the road "unless they're confident of their survival skills" or "Looking to be really lonely".

Ded Brenner fit both of those criteria.

He had been on the road for nine hours now and had seen maybe twenty motor vehicles, most of them were big rigs.

The 1962 Harley pan head grumbled away beneath him, eating up the miles just like it was designed to do. Brenner had purchased the bike many years ago and, over time, it had started to resemble a rat-bike rather than the original stock pan head. Kludged together from whatever was available at the time, painted matt black, and oil hungry, it seldom let him down. He had also replaced the tank for a larger one and had upgraded the shocks to carry more weight.

The upgraded shocks were a necessity as opposed to a luxury. After all, not only was Brenner a big man at six foot five inches and two hundred and seventy pounds, he also carried with him a twenty foot length of GR 100 alloy high strength steel chain and a massive SOBO high security shrouded padlock. This weighed in at another one hundred and ten pounds.

But he never went anywhere without it.

Never ever.

As he hit Missouri, Brenner started to notice the trees. Temperate broadleaves mixed with conifers. Sycamore, Cottonwood, Birch and Maple and Pines. But mainly White Oak and Shortleaf Pine. And when he got closer to the Ozarks and into the foothills of the mountains, the pine trees became the more prominent of the two.

As the trees started to shroud the road in shadow, Brenner realized that it was almost time. Official sunset was at seven twenty seven but twilight set in at around six twenty five. He glanced at his watch. Six o'clock. Scanning the land on the side of the highway he saw a dirt road up ahead, leaving the blacktop at an almost ninety degree angle.

He slowed down and took the turn, dropping two gears and bumping slowly along the dirt track. Within two miles the track almost petered out. This may have been a road to somewhere at one stage in its life, but now no one ever used it. Not for many years.

That suited Brenner just fine.

He pulled off the remnants of the track and rode slowly into the womb of the forest, deep enough so that he was no longer visible.

Then he kicked out his stand and climbed off the hog. After stretching he opened the right-hand saddlebag and took out his chain and padlock, carrying the one hundred and ten pounds of steel in one hand, like it was a mere piece of jewelry. Next, he selected a tree. A mature White Oak.

He dropped the pile of steel chain at the foot of the tree, took out a pack of Lucky Strike cigarettes and fired up.

'Gonna have to change brands soon,' he said to himself. 'Can't find these anymore.' After finishing the cigarette, he crushed it out under his boot and then proceeded to strip, placing his clothes into a neat pile next to the Harley.

Finally, completely naked, he chained himself to the tree, wrapping the steel around himself and the Oak twice and then closing the chain with the padlock. Then he threw the key at the bike. It landed on the ground next to it.

The chain wasn't very tight. But that was because Brenner knew exactly how much slack he would need. Too tight and it might hurt him. Too loose and he might wriggle out.

He needed just enough play to allow for the change. No more, no less.

He waited patiently while the sun dropped below the horizon.

And then the moon rose. Full and bright. Like a silver dollar in the cloudless night sky.

The chain snapped tight.

The tree shook.

And a howl rent the night air.

Deep, visceral and atavistic. The primal sound of an Alpha predator.

The call of the wild.

The sound of nightmares made real.

CHAPTER 3

Thomas Pinkerton was too stoned to see properly. But he didn't mind. He could do his job with his eyes closed. His operation was small. They all were. That was the way that the big boss wanted it run.

Lots of small units. Spread the risk, he told them. That way, if something went wrong, then you only lost a small percentage of your production as opposed to the whole whack.

Thomas couldn't care less as to the reasons. All that he cared about was the fact that he was making enough money to own a brand new Corvette and a Jeep patriot, have ten pairs of identical Air Jordan Premiums and enough crystal meth to suck up his nose so that he could maintain a high, constant enough to prevent ever tweaking. Okay, sometimes he crashed, took to his bed for a few days. But then he would juice up and get running again. Sharp. Ready for anything. Super successful.

And that was more than you could say about any other dude that had dropped out of school aged fourteen with absolutely no qualifications whatsoever.

His girlfriend, LaQuanda, lay on a small cot at the back of the trailer. She had been booty bumping since they had woken up that morning. Dissolving meth in water and then squirting it up her ass with a turkey baster. The girl was now so high that she couldn't stop talking. Like a fucking auctioneer on steroids.

Thomas measured out a beaker full of ethyl alcohol and transferred it into his plastic container that already contained ammonia nitrate, sodium hydroxide and pseudoephedrine. He twisted the cap and shook the bottle up, waiting for the solution to settle out.

He forgot to replace the cap on the gallon drum of ethyl alcohol.

LaQuanda got up off the cot and hunted around in her bag for a pack of cigarettes. Found it, took one out, placed it in between her lips and took out her lighter.

'Hey,' shouted Thomas. 'Are you crazy, bitch? You can't light up in here. You stupid or something? Put that fucking thing down.'

LaQuanda stared at Thomas for a full thirty seconds before she reacted. 'You some sort of asshole, Thomas,' she screamed. 'Talk about fucking up a girl's high. Anyways, you ain't the boss of me. I be the boss of me. I'm a strong independent woman and you can't tell me what I can or can't do. Fuck you.'

She spun the wheel on the Zippo.

The explosion was visible from seven miles away.

The force of the blast destroyed the Corvette and the Jeep.

Oddly enough, a single Nike Air Jordan Premium was blown clear of the destruction, landing in an Oak tree some fifty feet away. Unblemished apart from some minor smoke stains.

A Mockingbird tilted its head to one side and surveyed the shoe for a while. Then, after deciding that it was inedible, took wing and left.

CHAPTER 4

The chain was back in the saddlebag. It had held.

And now Brenner was back on the road, the seventy-four cubic inches of engine hammering away underneath him. He glanced down at his aftermarket sportster fuel gage and noticed that the gas was running low. As well as that he was starting to hear the odd knock from the engine. Nothing that serious but still it needed to be looked at before it resulted in some sort of catastrophic failure.

Up ahead he saw a sign pointing left off the highway. 'Cabintown'. Under that a hand-painted wooden sign that read Gas, Food, Cold Beer.

He took the turnoff and throttled back, carefully avoiding the potholes and detritus that was strewn across the road. Tree branches, road-kill and random pieces of trash.

A few miles later he came to the outskirts of the town. Clapboard houses going to wrack and ruin. Creepers, long grass. Some with mature trees growing through the roofs.

In the gardens the odd car. Up on bricks. Covered in dirt. Eaten by rust. Victims of nature's inexorable cancer. None of the vehicles were later than the nineteen sixties and some were even earlier models. DeSoto's and Plymouths.

As he got closer to the center of the town, the buildings grew in height and size. Hardware stores, tailors, a drug store. Even an opera house, its golden façade faded to dull yellow, the signage hanging skew, windows cracked and broken.

All the shops were boarded up, save a single premise in the center of the main street.

A ragged sign outside said, Bar. At one stage the word had been picked out with electric light bulbs but now it relied on the weak sun that dappled through the trees, speckling the sign with spots of shadow like a virulent skin disease.

The double doors were open and a light shone within.

Brenner stopped outside; kicked his stand out, dismounted and entered.

Two old men sat inside. One behind the bar and the other on a barstool on the patron's side of the counter. Both were dark skinned with long gray hair and blue eyes. Bushy gray beards, semi formal clothing. Open necked white shirts, dark suits, patent leather shoes. The clothes were neat and clean and so threadbare that you could almost pick out the individual strands of the weave.

Brenner nodded his greeting.

The men nodded back.

'What you like to drink, stranger?' Asked the one behind the bar. Except it came out more like, '*Wat two lak a dink, stay her?'*

Brenner hesitated as his ears adjusted to the vernacular. Then he asked. 'What you got?'

'Got shine,' answered the barman.

'Anything else?'

'What else is there?' countered the barman. 'It's good. I believe it to be a combination of corn, barley, rye.'

'You believe?' Asked Brenner.

The old man laughed. A sound like gravel being rolled around a baking tin. 'I know then. As I should, 'cause I made it.' He poured Brenner a glass full. 'This one be on the house.'

'Thank you, old timer. My name is Brenner. Ded Brenner.'

The barman stuck his hand out and shook. His grip was strong, his hand reduced to bone and tendon by old age. 'I be mister Bolin and the old curmudgeon propping up the bar on your side be mister Reeve. What can we do you for, mister Brenner?'

'I saw a sign on the highway. Said, Gas. I'm looking to fill up. Maybe get a bite to eat.'

'Cain't get no gas here, son,' said mister Reeve. 'Ain't been nothing of the sort for decades. That sign be as old as the Ark.'

'Cain't get no food neither,' added mister Bolin. 'On account of we don't have much and what we do have we eat ourselves. We got shine aplenty, though.'

Brenner smiled. 'Can I run my bike on it?'

Both of the old men laughed loud. 'Surely be, son. Surely be. But we don't sell no shine for no gas substitute. Best you get back on the highway and drive some twenty mile or so till you see a sign that directs you to the town of "Goodbye". Take a left and you find gas there. Cain't miss the place. There be a huge chicken farm next to the highway, you can smell the chicken shit for miles.'

'Thank you,' said Brenner as he held out his glass for another shot. 'Can I buy you gentlemen a drink?'

Mister Bolin shook his head. 'Your money ain't no good here, boy,' he said. 'You just rest your bones for a while then be on your way.'

'Thank you.'

They drank in silence for a while. Brenner savored the shine. It was good. Clean, no aftertaste. Mister Bolin was obviously an experienced distiller.

'So, boy,' said mister Reeve. 'How long you been afflicted?'

'With what?' Asked Brenner.

Mister Reeve shook his head. 'It's fine. You don't want to talk about it.'

'About what?' Insisted Brenner.

'The moon lives in the lining of your skin,' answered mister Reeve. 'Plain as the nose on your face.'

'You aren't scared?' Asked Brenner.

'I'm a good judge of character. So how long?'

Brenner thought for a while. He considered continuing to deny all knowledge. Plead ignorance. Tell the old timer that he was playing loony tunes and he should mind his own business.

But there was something about these two old men. These two ancients sitting and drinking shine in a bar in a ghost town in the middle of nowhere. It seemed to demand the truth. Or at least something close to the truth.

Like a priest in a confessional.

'Since Vietnam,' answered Brenner. 'Nineteen sixty. I was a Ranger. 75th. I got volunteered to a black ops group called the Bloodborn Project. They were trying to create some sort of super-soldier. Drugs, genetic enhancement. That sort of thing. I was about to bug out when I got tagged in a firefight in *Ia Drang*. Shot to bits. Took six shots to the chest. I woke up a few weeks later in some underground hospital. Laboratory, actually. Next thing I know, I'm a fucking werewolf. Now I search the country for a cure for this curse. Something to stop me becoming a raving, killing beast on the first day of every full moon.'

'We been living in these here mountains for a long time, mister Wolf Brenner,' said mister Bolin. 'A long time. And we have a saying; a mountain with a wolf on it stands a little bit higher. Perhaps it isn't the curse that you think it is.'

'Anyway,' added mister Reeve. 'Ain't no cure for being what you are. You just are and you gotta live with it boy. You can't change what you can't change and that's that.'

Brenner put his empty glass down. 'Thanks for the shine, misters,' he said. 'I better be heading off. You take care now.'

They both nodded at Brenner as he walked out. When he got to the door, mister Reeve called out to him. 'You are what you are, boy. Learn to live with it. You are what you are.'

Brenner mounted his bike and turned the ignition. The engine rumbled to life.

A dust devil skittered across the street, flirting with the sidewalk like a drunken dancer until it collapsed in on itself. Dying in full view of the abandoned buildings. The broken windows. The empty street.

Somewhere, right on the very edge of his hearing, Brenner swore that he could hear some people singing. A church choir. People crying softly in the background. A funeral?

Perhaps it was just the wind.

He gunned the throttle and spun out of the town, bumping and jolting on the rough road.

CHAPTER 5

The two old misters were right, Brenner could smell the chicken farm long before he saw it. The stench of thousands of living creatures crammed into an area probably more suited to house mere hundreds.

Twenty, massive, low buildings made from steel and polycarbonate. Like third world aircraft hangers. On the side, a huge selection of stainless steel food and water hoppers. Smoke from some sort of disposal unit filled the air and the greasy stink stuck at the back of Brenner's throat. It was like some sort of poultry concentration camp.

The town of Goodbye hove into view as he passed the poultry extermination factory.

It was like riding onto Pleasantville USA - Leave it to Beaver. White picket fences, perfectly trimmed lawns, a red-and-white barber pole.

Up on a hill overlooking the town, a large faux Antebellum mansion with Greek Ionic columns, Georgian dimensions and Victorian Gothic. Lifestyles of the rich and tasteless. Brenner shook his head.

He rode past a service station, outside two old-fashioned gas pumps, the double doors were closed and it was obvious that no one was there so he continued on to the diner. A poem in neon and chrome and glass. A sign above read, Betty's Diner.

He kicked out his stand, dismounted and entered. The place was well lit and around half of the tables were taken. He picked a stool at the counter top, sat and waited for attention. There was a man behind the griddle and a blonde woman behind the counter. She was polishing glasses and every few seconds she would glance up at him and then her eyes would flick down and she would continue at her task.

Finally Brenner spoke. 'Excuse me, ma'am,' he said. The girl flushed up but didn't look at him. Brenner glanced around the room and noticed that everybody else was also studiously ignoring him.

Just then a police car pulled up outside and two deputies walked in. Both slightly breathless. They walked straight up to Brenner and stood real close. Invading his personal space. An obvious intimidation tactic. They were both young, meat fed, gym trained. A match for Brenner in height and probably shading him by twenty pounds each. These were big men. The kind of big that you seldom saw outside of the WWE or a professional football field.

Brenner managed not to laugh.

'You lookin' for something, boy?' Asked the one.

Brenner glanced at the man's name tag before he

spoke. 'Well, deputy Kennedy,' he said. 'A little service would go a long way. Figured on some coffee and something to eat.'

The two of them mouth-breathed a bit before Kennedy spoke again. 'Fair enough,' he said. 'I reckon that you can get yourself a bite to eat and then you be on your way.'

'That what you reckon?' confirmed Brenner.

Kennedy nodded and then he gestured to the girl behind the counter. 'Betty. Serve the man.'

She walked over, a nervous smile plastered across her face. 'What can I get you, stranger?'

Brenner smiled. 'Coffee, black. Loads of sugar. I like sugar. And a plate full of food. What do you recommend?'

'We do a mean mixed grill,' observed Betty. 'Chicken, sausage, steak, kidneys, bacon, corn, mash potato and slaw.'

'Fix me two of those,' said Brenner.

'It's an awful big serving, mister.'

'That's good, because I'm awful hungry.'

Betty nodded and turned to the cook. 'Boisy, gimme two bean busters, all the way.'

The cook saluted her with a spatula and got to frying.

The two deputies continued to stand right next to Brenner, leaning slightly towards him, mouths open and sneers on their faces.

Brenner grinned. 'You boys want to back off a little. Give a man some breathing room?'

'We stand were we want,' said the second deputy.

Brenner glanced at his name tag. 'Seriously,' he said. 'Smelly?'

'It's pronounced Smeelie,' countered the steroid monster.

'What's the R stand for?' Asked Brenner.

'Richard.'

Brenner started to laugh. 'Really. Richard. Dick. Your name is Dick Smelly?'

The deputy went bright red and started to breathe heavily. Then he grabbed Brenner by the forearm.

The room went silent and Betty cringed away from them, her face screwed up in anticipation.

Brenner didn't move. He simply looked at Smelly, his golden eyes unblinking, his posture relaxed but alert. Then he shook his head. A tiny almost unnoticeable movement. And, under his breath he said one word, softly spoken but carrying with it an unspoken threat of unimaginable violence. 'No.'

And Smelly found himself looking into the abyss.

He jerked his arm back as if he had been scalded, his face pale, his breathing shallow. Then without uttering another word he turned on his heel and left the diner.

Kennedy gave Brenner a puzzled look and then followed his partner. Moments later their car spun out of the parking lot.

In the diner the noise level went back to normal.

Betty arrived with Brenner's coffee and she set it down in front of him.

'What was that all about?' Asked Betty. 'Never

seen Dick back down from a confrontation before.'

Brenner shrugged. 'No idea. He must have wanted to see a man about a dog.'

Betty laughed. 'You're funny.'

'Hilarious,' agreed Brenner.

She stuck her hand out. 'I'm Betty. Betty Parker. This is my diner.'

Brenner shook her hand. It was small. Tiny. But not soft. Strong. Calluses and rough skin. Real hands. Dishwashing hands. Cooking hands. Cleaning hands. The hands of a proper hard working American girl.

'My name is Brenner. Ded Brenner.'

'Dead?'

'Officially it's short for Dedreck. My mother's family name. But when my father registered the birth he just forgot three consonants and a vowel. Anyhow, most folks just call me Brenner.'

'Betty,' the cook called. 'Two bean busters.'

Betty picked up the two plates of food and deposited them in front of Brenner. She was correct. The portions were huge. Gigantic.

Brenner set to, wolfing the food down like an industrial disposal unit. Within minutes the first plate was empty, and he sat back to savor the second, asking for more coffee as he did so.

'Damn this is good,' he said.

Betty grinned. 'It's my brother. Boisy. He's a genius when it comes to meat.'

Brenner waved at Boisy. 'Compliments to the chef,' he said.

Boisy stared at him for a few seconds and then shrugged.

'He says the food is good, Boisy,' said Betty.

Boisy grinned widely and saluted Brenner. 'Thank you, sir,' he said. 'Boisy tries his best he does. Boisy tries his best, always.'

'He doesn't know words like compliments,' explained Betty. 'Not even sure he knows the word, chef.'

'Why?'

'He has IDD,' explained Betty.

'What?'

'IDD. Intellectual Disability Disorder.'

'I see,' said Brenner hesitantly.

Betty laughed. 'It's new-speak for retard,' she said. 'My granny used to call him feeble minded, my mama said he was mentally retarded and now we gotta say that he as an intellectual disability disorder. The deputies just call him the Retard or just Tard.'

'Well the deputies are assholes,' said Brenner.

Betty glanced around the room before she agreed.

Brenner finished his second plateful and downed his coffee. 'Thanks, Betty,' he said. 'Now, truth be told, I simply need a tank of gas and then I'll be heading on my way. Looks like the local law enforcement haven't taken too kindly to me at any rate so I might as well be moving on.'

Betty frowned. 'Look, Brenner, there's no way you'll get any gas on the weekend. The Johansen bothers go out of town every weekend and they own the gas station. Soonest you'll get is Monday morning.'

'Shit,' said Brenner.

'Look,' continued Betty. 'There ain't no hotel or nothing here but I'm sure that you could rent a room off Doc Morrison. He's not a real doctor. I think he's some sort of dinosaur doctor. Like a real intellectual type. He's got a room spare and I reckon he needs the money. He retired here some two years back with his wife and...' Betty hesitated. 'Well, with his wife.'

'Where is he?'

'Down the high street, first left, first right. Two story house, roses on the fence. Tell him that Betty said to call.'

Brenner stood up. 'Thanks, Betty. What do I owe you?'

'That'll be twelve dollars.'

Brenner raised an eyebrow. 'Twelve dollars? What happened, I take a time machine back to the sixties?'

'Twelve dollars,' repeated Betty.

Brenner took out a billfold and placed twenty dollars on the counter. 'Keep the change for Boisy,' he said as he walked out.

Betty watched him leave. As did all the other patrons in the establishment. And it was as if everyone let out a sigh of relief at the same time. Shoulders lowered, hands unclenched and breathing slowed. Like a man eating tiger had strolled through the room and then decided, not today, I'm full. But maybe tomorrow I'll be back. There was a general feeling of reprieve. A stay of execution.

In the corner an old man beckoned to Betty with his empty coffee cup. She went over to offer a refill.

'Who was that man?' Asked the old timer.

'His name's, Brenner,' answered Betty. 'Why?'

The old man shook his head. 'Back in the day I met a man like him. In Vietnam. Special Forces. And until today that was the scariest human being that I had ever come across. Well, I guess I can't say that anymore.'

He raised the coffee to his lips with a trembling hand and took a sip, his eyes misty with memory.

CHAPTER 6

Brenner parked his Harley outside the house that Betty had given him directions to. It was a standard clapboard double story structure with a screened porch. As Betty had said, there were climbing roses on the white picket fence. Red and yellow. They had been neglected and were starting to revert to the wild. But the lawn was well trimmed, and the house gleamed with a coat of new white paint. Brenner walked up to the front door and knocked.

Ages later a man shuffled up and opened the door. He was much younger than Brenner had expected. Maybe mid to late thirties. But his eyes were older. Peering out above a set of steel rimmed, round eyeglasses. A blue so pale as to be almost a cloudy white. He wore the uniform of the academic. Cotton trousers, a button down shirt and a tweed jacket with leather patches on the elbows. On his feet, carpet slippers. A thirty-five-year old man dressed for Halloween as an octogenarian grandpa.

He simply stared at Brenner without greeting.

His hand on the door handle. His eyeglasses slipping slowly down his nose.

'Are you Doc Morrison?'

The man nodded.

'Betty sent me. I'm just passing through and she said that you might be kind enough to rent me a room for a couple of days. Just until Monday morning when I can gas up and get on my way.'

'A room?'

Brenner nodded.

'Yes,' affirmed the Doc. 'I have a spare room. No use for it now.'

'Excellent,' said Brenner. 'Could I stay for two nights?' He took out his billfold. 'I can pay up front. Should we say sixty dollars?' He peeled off six ten dollar notes and proffered them.

The Doc stared at them for a few seconds. Almost as if he were unaware as to what they were. Then his hand snatched at them and he pushed the unfolded notes into his trouser pocket. 'Downstairs,' he said. 'Follow me.'

'Great,' said Brenner. 'Let me grab my kit and I'll be right behind you.'

The Doc showed him to a room in the basement. It had a head height window along the one wall, thick carpets, a double bed, dresser and free standing cupboard. In the corner a shower. Although the room was fairly sparse and painted all in white, it somehow gave off a vaguely feminine air. As if a young girl had started decorating it and then lost interest in a day. It smelled of new paint.

'You can use the toilet off the passage on the first floor. Please don't go upstairs to the second floor. There's coffee in the kitchen. It's instant. We only have soya milk.'

'Thanks, Doc.'

The young old man waved his hand vaguely in the air and shuffled out of the room, closing the door behind him.

Brenner took the time to have a shower. The water dribbled out like someone was wringing a wet cloth over him, but it was wet and warm. Then he dried himself and put on a fresh shirt, boxers, jeans, boots. He decided to go upstairs and avail himself of some of the Docs instant coffee.

Morrison was sitting at the kitchen table. In front of him a steaming mug of tea, English style with milk and sugar. Brenner nodded, spotted the coffee and ladled a few spoonfuls into a mug. He checked that the water was still hot, filled the mug and then spooned in a generous amount of sugar.

He sat opposite the Doc. As he took a sip, he noticed an ashtray on the table. It had a couple of butts in.

'You smoke?' He asked the Doc.

'Yes.'

Brenner took out a pack of Lucky Strike. 'Do you mind?'

The Doc shook his head. Brenner offered, and he accepted. Then Brenner took one himself, flicked his Zippo and lit the Doc up first.

'My father used to smoke these,' said the Doc.

'Didn't know that they still made them.'

'I don't think that they do,' said Brenner. 'Well, not here, in the States anymore. I'm finding them more difficult to get hold of every day. But it's what I always smoked so, old habits die hard.'

They sat for a while in companionable silence. Brenner broke it with a question.

'So, what are you a doctor of?'

'I'm not a medical doctor, if that's what you were wondering,' answered Morrison. 'The real town doctor lives three houses down. He's an old soak called Doctor Hoffman. The town clinic is attached to his home. There's no hospital. You get sick, you go to Hoffman's sanatorium. I'm a paleontologist.'

'Dinosaurs,' observed Brenner.

'Actually, plants mainly. Ancient flora. I also have a doctorate in pure mathematics.'

'And now, what do you do?'

'Nothing,' breathed the Doc. 'I used to lecture. Back east. But then Shelly got ill and everything went to shit.'

'Shelly?'

'My wife. She's upstairs. Eventually our medical insurance ran dry. We sold the house, cars, cashed in my pension. When we had nothing left, we moved here. My aunt left us this place. I'd sell this too if I could, but who wants to buy a house in Buttfuck, Missouri?'

'I don't know,' admitted Brenner. 'But the town seems alright. It's clean and well maintained. Some might even say it's idyllic.'

'Some might,' concurred the Doc. 'But some might be wrong.'

Brenner didn't argue. 'So what's wrong with your wife?'

'Prions disease. There isn't really a cure. Hell, some people even claim that it isn't actually a disease. Fuck them. We are trying a raft of drugs. Some experimental. That's why the insurance won't pay. She gets weaker every day. But they said that she wouldn't last a year. That was three years ago.'

'I'm sorry,' said Brenner.

'Not your fault.'

Brenner shrugged and stood up. 'Thanks for the coffee, Doc. I know that it's early but I've been on the road for a while now and I find that I should take sleep when I can get it. I bid you goodnight.'

The Doc nodded but remained seated, staring blankly into space.

***

The next morning Brenner woke early. He glanced at his watch and saw with surprise that it was six in the morning. He had slept for twelve hours straight. He showered and headed for the front door. On the way out he noticed an open carton with a UPS label on. Next to it was an invoice. A list of drugs. At the bottom the total in dollars.

Four thousand.

Brenner wondered how the hell the Doc was going to pay for that.

As it was a sunny day, and he wanted to stretch his legs, he decided to walk to the diner for breakfast. But he took the long route. Cutting right so that he could walk to the end of the town and then down the whole length of the main street.

Once again he was impressed at the general order of the place. Like a brochure for America's perfect town.

The fire station was a bright, gleaming affair and Brenner noted that it had three new looking fire trucks. Two tankers and an aerial ladder truck. Enough for a town five times the size of Goodbye.

Two buildings away was the sheriff's office. Another building that was incongruously large for the size of the community that it served. Brenner figured on maybe enough space for twenty deputies with appropriate support staff. For a town that needed no more than two deputies and the sheriff.

'Curiouser and curiouser,' mumbled Brenner to himself.

Despite the relatively early hour, the diner was once again over half full.

Brenner took the same seat at the counter and waited for Betty. She approached with a smile, a cup of coffee and a sugar pourer.

'Betty.'

'Brenner. What can I do you for?'

'Food,' smiled Brenner. 'Loads.'

'Loads of food coming right up, sir.' She turned to holler at Boisy. 'Give me two belly busters, stat.'

The young man saluted and threw some lard on the griddle, working it hard with his spatula to get a nice smooth finish. Then he started to pile his wares on. Hamburger, link sausages, tomatoes, mushrooms, fried bread, eggs and bacon.

Minutes later Brenner had enough food in front of him to feed a troop of boy scouts. Once again he set to. When he was finished, he slapped a twenty down, stood up, waved to Betty and went out for a leisurely walk and a Lucky Strike. No sooner had he lit up when a police car pulled up next to him.

The window slid down to reveal his two favorite deputies.

'Hey,' said Brenner. 'It's the Chuckle Brothers. To what do I owe the pleasure?'

The doors opened and the two of them stepped out.

'I thought that we had an agreement,' said Kennedy. 'You eat, you leave.'

Brenner made a pretense at thinking, then he spoke. 'No, sorry,' he shook his head. 'Don't recall that.'

'Yesterday, dipshit. We said that you could have a bite to eat and then you make your way out of town.'

'Can't,' said Brenner. 'No gas. Have to wait until Monday. For the service station to open up.'

'Well where are you staying then?' Asked Kennedy.

'Doc Morrison.'

'Fine,' interjected Smelly. 'Then get yourself back

there right now. We don't want to see you on the streets.'

Brenner thought before he answered. He was only going to be in this unfriendly shithole for one more day and night. There was no need to make waves. Common sense dictated that he simply walk back to the Docs, lie low and leave the next morning.

So he said. 'Fuck you, Smelly Dick.'

Smelly put his hand on his revolver, flipping the thumb break open as he did so. 'Insulting a police officer and obstructing justice,' he shouted at Brenner. 'I got you now, you big city fuck. You're under arrest.'

Brenner felt the hair on the back of his neck stand up and his muscles start to bunch and swell. At the same time his teeth started to extend and his fingers nails thicken up. With a huge effort of will he stopped the process, crushing down his anger. He shook his head. 'You better make sure that your next move is the right one, partner,' he growled at Smelly. 'Otherwise I swear to the lord that you will be wearing your own ass as a hat when I'm finished with you.'

Before either of the deputies could react, another car pulled up next to them and the driver window rolled down. Inside sat a large man with silver hair. Rolls of fat bulked up under his chin to make a pillow of lard and his shirt strained to keep everything tightly controlled. His eyes were blue and set close together, high up in his face like they were trying to avoid his nose. He was sweating profusely in spite of the glacial air-conditioning in the car.

On his shirt, a single gold star that read, Sherriff.

'What seems to be the problem, boys?'

'Nothing, Sherriff,' answer Smelly. 'Just arresting this asshole for insulting a police officer.'

'Insulting a police officer?' enquired the sheriff.

'Yes, sir.'

The sheriff laughed. 'Hell, boy, you can't arrest someone for that. Shit, I believe that it's actually mandatory to insult police officers in some states.'

'Sir,' said Smelly. 'He said he would make me wear my ass as a hat, sir.'

The sheriff laughed again. 'Richard. Give it a rest. Get back in the car and go and do your actual job. You too, Ken.'

'But, sir,' argued Smelly.

The sheriff stopped laughing and his eyes glittered with anger. 'Richard,' he said. 'Fuck off. Now.'

Both of the deputies scuttled back to their car and took off. The sheriff turned to Brenner. 'Jump in,' he said. 'We'll go to the station, drink some coffee. Have a little chat.'

Brenner shook his head. 'It's okay, sheriff,' he said. 'I'll just be getting on my way. No worries.'

The sheriff sighed. 'It's not a request, son,' he said. 'Now get in car before I get upset.'

Brenner walked around to the passenger side, opened the door and got in. It was like walking into a blast freezer.

The sheriff drove to the station in silence and pulled up outside. Brenner followed him in to discover that the interior was also air-conditioned to within an inch of its life. You could carry out autopsies in the place and the bodies wouldn't spoil for weeks.

The deputy on duty greeted the sheriff when he entered as did some of the support staff. He ignored then as if they weren't there. Brenner followed him as he waddled across the room to his office. He opened the door and ushered Brenner in.

It was a standard sheriff's office except for the fact that it was a little larger than normal. Also, the furnishings and fixtures were more upmarket. A governor's office as opposed to a sheriff's.

The red, white and blue Missouri flag covered the wall behind the desk. On the other wall a large scale map of the area. Opposite that a picture window and across the last wall, a wet bar. On the bar stood a Bunn flask of coffee. It smelled fresh.

The sheriff poured a cup of coffee for each of them and sat down, gesturing for Brenner to sit opposite him. He didn't offer sugar and Brenner couldn't see any so he didn't bother to ask, instead he drank the coffee like medicine.

'So,' said the sheriff. 'I be Alec Goins. The sheriff of Goodbye. And you?'

'Ded Brenner.'

Goins nodded. 'Talk to me, Brenner.'

'Nothing to say, sheriff. I'm going from one place to another place. Ran out of gas, stopped for a refill and discovered that I had to wait until Monday to do so.'

'Where exactly you heading?'

'Some place that isn't here.'

The sheriff smiled. Or, to put it more accurately, he exposed his teeth. But his little piggy eyes showed no emotional response to his facial expression. 'You sparring with me, son?'

'No, sir.'

'Good. We started on a good footing here. No reason to ruin things by developing a smart attitude. Agreed?'

Brenner nodded. He had met men like this before. Dangerous men. Men that used cruelty as a form of discipline. That masked hatred as firmness. And saw compassion as a weakness. Small men with big ambitions.

'So tell me, Brenner. What did you do to get my deputies so hot under the collar?'

Brenner smiled. 'Called him Smelly Dick.'

Goins slapped his thigh and burst out laughing. 'No wonder. Surprised that he let you get away with it though. Richard is a mite touchy about his name and he tends to back up his displeasure with over three hundred pounds of pissed off.'

Brenner shrugged. 'I have a way with words. Convinced him that he had better things to do than take his frustrations out on me.'

'Yep, I was here at the station when he got back from his... discussion with you yesterday. Never seen the boy so het up and yet so goddam terrified at the same time.'

'Terrified?'

Goins nodded. 'Pale as a sheet, hands shaking. I know fear, son. I know it well. And what I saw on Richard's face was pure and unadulterated. Now why do you suppose that is?'

Brenner shrugged. 'Maybe he has a phobia of some sort.'

Goins nodded. 'Maybe. Maybe.' He stared at Brenner for a while. Unblinking.

Brenner stared back.

No one spoke for a full minute. And then Brenner loosened the leash slightly. Unhooding his eyes and letting the predator inside take a peek out.

Goins started to sweat even more than before. 'I see,' he said. As he stood up. 'I want you gone first thing tomorrow morning, Brenner. I'll get word to the brothers to open at sunrise. You fill your tank and get out of my town. We clear?'

'Crystal.'

'You know the way out,' said Goins.

He didn't say goodbye or offer his hand.

Neither did Brenner.

CHAPTER 7

Brenner lay on the bed and stared at the ceiling. There was a lot wrong with this little town in the middle of nowhere. A lot wrong.

'So what?' He asked himself. 'It has nothing to do with me. Sleep, wake up. Gas up and fuck off. Never think about the town of Goodbye again. Never think of the Chuckle Brothers. Or the dangerous sheriff. Or Betty. Or Boisy the meat master with his IDD. Forget about the deputies that called the kid a retard. And the overlarge fire station. And the sheriff's office big enough for a town of over a hundred thousand people.'

Just forget about it.

'Shit.' He put his boots on and headed for the front door. 'Just a quick scout around,' he said to himself. 'Put my mind at ease.'

As he was about to open the front door he stopped. Tilted his head to one side. Sniffed the air. Smiled. The Chuckle Brothers. Twenty, maybe twenty-five feet away. He turned and left via the back door, moving silently. Sticking to the shadows, blending into the night. Becoming the darkness.

He slid past the two deputies, close enough to touch them if he wanted to, his body more shadow than flesh. A skill learned in the jungles of Vietnam and then honed by his curse. Or his gift if the two moonshine drinking old men in the bar were to be believed. He was tempted to tie Smelly's shoelaces together but decided against it.

Instead, he jogged to the outskirts of the town.

As soon as he hit the beginnings of the forest he stopped, found a secluded spot and stripped down, folding his clothes and piling them neatly in the fork of a tree.

Then he changed. It was nothing like the movies. There was no grinding of bones as he grew, no rending of flesh. It was a thing of beauty. A swift metamorphosis from man to beast.

And there he stood. Dark gray with a pale belly. Fur thick and healthy. The same eyes. A wolf, fully as large as a horse.

He ran.

Twenty minutes later he returned. He had done a circuit of the town and taken a small deviation to the chicken farm and had seen nothing overtly suspicious apart from the usual fact. The town was far too prosperous for its size. The inhabitants were too well off. The public services were disproportionately large.

The chicken farm proved to be the usual nightmare of modern mass production farming. They obviously used a shit house full of ammonia hydroxide liquid because there were hundreds of drums of it stacked outside the offices. In the back of his mind he seemed to remember that it was used to kill the pathogens in the meat. Or something. *Man*, he thought to himself, *who would eat the shit that came out of these mass production chicken farms?*

Also, there were more people living in trailer homes than he would have thought. He had seen many of them, scattered around, off in the distance. But even they were well cared for, clean and modern looking with small gardens and children's play areas.

No law against any of that, thought Brenner. None at all.

He morphed into human form; put his clothes on and headed back to the Doc's, coming from the opposite end of town that he had left from.

As he passed the diner he heard voices, and he melted into the scenery as he moved to the rear of the building to see who was there. At the back of the diner was a conjoined house. In the doorway stood Betty. On the porch, Smelly. He hulked there like a bear. Legs apart, stance aggressive. Jaw stuck out in a pugnacious expression.

'I'm fine, Richard,' said Betty, her voice slightly shaky.

'I think that I better come inside and check,' answered Smelly. 'You never know. Tonight could be the night that the retard loses his shit and kills you in your sleep.'

'He's not like that, Richard. He's not violent.'

'Whatever. Just might be that I should come in, show my face. Maybe discipline him a little just to make sure that he knows to behave himself.'

'No, Richard,' said Betty. 'Please. I'm fine. Everything is fine. Please go.'

Smelly stepped forward into the doorway. 'Maybe after I discipline the retard, you can show me a bit of appreciation. Maybe.' He pushed her back into the house hard enough to send her sprawling across the floor.

She stood up as fast as she could, a tear rolling down her one cheek.

Then they heard the growl. Its amplitude so high that the windows and the screen doors shivered in concert. The top of the food chain had spoken, and all around shivered in fear.

And Smelly simply disappeared. Yanked back like someone had tied a rope to him and then attached it to a monster truck and driven off at maximum speed.

Betty watched him as he flew through the air and smashed up against a tree some seventy feet away. Even at that distance the sounds of crunching bones were plainly audible.

Then she saw a flicker of a shadow and something huge vanished into the night.

Hesitantly, she walked over to Smelly's prone body. Both of his legs were twisted so that the feet looked like they had been put on backwards and his right arm was bent at an impossible angle.

Blood poured from his nose and ears, but he was still breathing.

She smiled, gave him a quick kick in the ribs and then went back inside to call the sheriff.

CHAPTER 8

The black BMW 740iL pulled up in front of the biker bar. The neon light flickered in the night sky. 'Aunty Murphy's bar'. Outside the front entrance at least fifty Harley's were lined up. Like steel horses at the rail.

Sergeant Solomon Hopewell sat in the back of the limousine. He opened a briefcase on the seat next to him. Inside were thirty small syringes with needles attached. Each one was filled with a deep red, viscous liquid. Three a day. Ten days supply. Solomon pulled the protective cap off one, tapped it to ensure there were no air bubbles and then stuck it deep into his neck and pushed the plunger.

He shivered as the serum coursed through his veins, boosting his strength, his speed and his healing abilities. Keeping him alive.

As soon as the tremors stopped he stepped out of the back of the limousine and went to the driver's window. 'Wait. I shouldn't be long.'

'Will you need any help, mister Solomon?' Asked corporal Howard, the driver.

Solomon laughed. 'I hardly think so,' he said.

'There can't be much more than fifty or sixty of them.'

He went up the steps and through the double doors into the saloon. The main theme of the bar seemed to be Confederate flag meets big game hunter. There must have been at least a hundred stuffed heads. Deer, bear, wolf, coyote, boar. And in between the heads hung the Dixie flag in every size imaginable.

The juke box hammered out Lynyrd Skynyrd at speaker distorting volume and the lights were low.

The bulk of the men in the room were gathered around a pro-arm-wrestling table. Standing opposite each other at the table stood two men. Both as big as Mack trucks. Shaven heads, cut off denim jackets and attitude to spare.

Solomon was wearing his customary black suit. Thin black leather gloves. Black leather Trilby hat. Dark aviator sunglasses. His skin so pale it looked as though he had applied white makeup. Like a clown without the jolly bits. No reds and blues and no false nose.

Everybody stopped what they were doing and stared.

He smiled. 'Carry on, gentlemen. As you were.' Then he walked over to the bar and pulled out a photograph. He flashed it at the barman.

It was an old photo. Faded but clear enough to make out the man's features. He wore Vietnam era combat dress. Sleeves cut off. A helmet. In the headband a pack of Lucky Strike cigarettes.

'You seen this man?' He asked. 'Rides a sixty two pan head. Black. A bit ratty.'

The barman's expression didn't change. 'What you drinking?'

'Whisky. Scottish.'

'We only serve American, project runway,' retorted the barman. 'Wild Turkey or Jack?'

'Jack then. Seen him?' Solomon held up the photo again.

The barman shrugged. 'Seen lots like him. But if that's an original photo the dude would be around eighty years old. What gives?'

Solomon tossed the Jack back and gestured for another. 'Seen him?' He repeated.

'No,' answered the barman. 'Maybe the guys have. Not me, I serve drinks, I see nothing. Ever.'

Solomon tossed the next drink back and wondered over to the crowd of arm wrestling watchers. He held out the photo. 'Any of you gentlemen seen this dude?'

'Fuck off,' said one of the Mack trucks.

'That's not polite, fat boy,' retorted Solomon.

'Who's your fat boy, Michael Jackson? You want to ask questions? Then play or fuck off.' He gestured to the table.

Solomon sighed and went to stand opposite the man-mountain. 'Fine,' he said. 'But after I win, I want answers.'

The crowd laughed.

'In your dreams, Johnny Cash.'

The mountain presented his hand and Solomon

gripped.

Another biker stepped forward, older man, gray beard. 'Right, gents. One foot in contact with the floor at all times. Non pulling hand must stay in contact with the peg. Ready?'

Solomon nodded.

'Just call it, Gunther,' shouted the mountain.

The referee nodded. 'Okay, Carl. Hold your horses. Gentlemen, close your thumbs. Go.'

The mountain screamed out a war cry and threw everything he had at Solomon, hoping to smash his hand down in ultimate humiliation. Give the biker boys someone and something to laugh at. But Solomon's expression didn't even change. Not even a blink. He simply stood there like he was holding an ice cream cone in his hand as opposed to wrestling a four hundred pound semi-human being.

The mountain started to sweat as the lactose acid built up in his muscles, eating away his energy. His strength.

Solomon winked. And then he pushed back

The Mack truck's arm snapped with a sound like a gunshot. The ragged ends of both the ulna and the radius punched through the flesh on his forearm like two sharp sticks.

Carl squealed like a stuck pig as he sank to the floor and, mercifully, passed out.

Solomon held up the photo once again. 'Have any of you seen this man?'

The sound of a shotgun being racked cut through

the silence. Then the click of a switchblade being readied for combat.

'I think that you should leave,' advised the referee.

Solomon smiled. There was a blur of movement as he attacked the shotgun wielder, ripping the weapon out of his hands, striking the man on the temple with the butt and throwing it through the window into the parking area outside. Then, as if the entire episode was being filmed in stop motion photography, he blurred into movement again, plucked the switchblade out of the next man's hand, smashed his elbow into his nose with a sound like a boot on gravel and threw the knife underhand so that it pegged into the exact center of the dartboard hanging on the far wall.

He grabbed Gunther, the referee, and held the photo in front of his face. 'Have you seen him?'

Gunther nodded frantically. 'Yep. Don't kill me. He was here six days ago. Didn't speak to no one. Ate, drank left.'

'You sure that it was him?'

Gunther nodded again. 'I'm real sure. You don't forget a man like him. It was like he walked in darkness. Always in the shadows, like they followed him. He was real scary.'

Solomon smiled. 'Scarier than me?'

The man closed his eyes tight and didn't answer.

'Scarier than me?' Repeated Solomon. 'Tell the truth. For the truth shall set you free.'

Gunther nodded again. 'God help me, yes. He was

scarier than even you. Please don't hurt me.'

Solomon smiled. 'That's him,' he said. He struck the old man once with his right fist. A short sharp blow that crushed his nose and shattered his cheek bones. Then he let him drop to the floor as he pointed at the barman.

'And you.'

The barman flinched in fear.

'You better get some decent fucking whisky. Scotch. Single malt. Preferably from the lowlands. Because if I come back here for any reason and you don't have an acceptable drink for me. Well then, I just might get a little pissed off.'

Solomon left at speed, a mere blur of light.

No one spoke for at least three minutes.

CHAPTER 9

Monday morning. Brenner was the first into the diner. Five thirty in the morning.

'Betty.'

'Hey, Brenner.' She smiled.

'You look in good spirits for this time of day,' noted Brenner.

Betty laughed. 'I love the mornings. Everything feels so clean. The air is fresh. A new sun. A new day. A new beginning. Same as yesterday?'

'Same again,' agreed Brenner.

Betty called the order out and brought coffee.

As she served up the breakfast, deputy Kennedy walked in and came straight over to Brenner.

'Times up, boy,' he said. 'Gas up and get the hell out.'

Brenner didn't even look at him. 'Eating,' he said. 'Fuck off. Anyway, where's the other Chuckle Brother?'

'Not that it has anything to do with you, asshole,' replied Kennedy. 'But he's ill. Resting up.'

'Oh really? That's a shame. Hope that he recovers real soon.'

'He will,' assured Kennedy. 'He's tough.'

Brenner shook his head. 'Not so sure, man,' he disagreed. 'Those compound fractures are a bitch. May be that he never gets out of bed again. May be.'

Kennedy reacted instantly, stepping back and drawing his revolver. 'How did you know that he had a fractured leg?' He shouted. 'Who told you?'

Betty rushed forwards. 'Stop it, Kenny,' she said. 'I did. I'm sorry. I didn't know that it was meant to be a secret.'

Kennedy holstered his weapon. 'It's not, Betty,' he admitted. 'It's just that I don't think that you should be talking to this drifter. He's no good.'

'No worries, Kenny,' said Brenner. 'I'll finish up and be out of here. Wouldn't want to take a chance with such a quick draw expert protecting the town. Wow, a real life Billy the Kid.'

Kennedy shook his head as he walked out. 'Asshole,' he mumbled under his breath.

Betty stood next to Brenner for a while and then she put her hand on his arm. 'It was you,' she said.

'Might have been,' admitted Brenner. 'That asshat come visiting often or was that the first time?'

Betty nodded. 'Often enough. I try to keep things quiet when he does. I don't want him to hurt Boisy.'

'Son of a bitch,' said Brenner. 'I should have killed the bastard.' There was silence for a few seconds. Then he spoke again. 'In fact I will kill him. Does the sheriff know?'

'Yes.'

'He's a dead man as well.'

Betty shook her head and stroked Brenner's arm. 'No,' she said. 'You have no idea what is going on.'

'Then tell me.'

'No. You've done enough. Thank you. Now it's time to leave before things escalate and we all suffer.'

'You happy here?' Asked Brenner.

'That's not the point. I live. And I live better than most in this country of ours. I can take care of Boisy, I make enough to cover his medical expenses. I'm okay. Please, Brenner, don't try to fix something that isn't broken. You wanna charge in here like a knight in shining armor and save us peasants but you never asked if we wanted to be saved. If we even need to be saved. You done enough.' She leaned forward and kissed him on the lips. 'Thank you Ded Brenner. I doubt that I'll be getting any unwanted visitors for a while now. It's over. Now go before things get bad.'

Brenner stood up and placed a hundred dollars on the counter. 'For Boisy,' he said. And he left without looking back.

***

'It's Brenner, sheriff. I can feel it in my gut. I mean, why is he here?'

'No mystery there, Kenny,' answered Goins. 'He ran out of gas.'

'Really? I bit convenient don't you think? He runs out of gas and now Richard is a fucking cripple. The doctor says that he might never walk the same again. Leg's broke in twenty seven places. He's lucky that they didn't amputate it.'

'You can't blame that on Brenner.'

'Then who, sheriff? I'm telling you, that son bitch sucker punched Richard. Ain't nothing like that happened before he pitched up. Must be him.'

Goins thought for a while. 'You know, Kenny,' he said. 'Just because you're paranoid doesn't necessarily mean that they're not out to get you. You could be right. Don't see no other explanation. The Lord knows that no one else around here would be ballsy or stupid enough to take on Richard. Even if you win, you don't win. And I do believe that an injury to one of us is an injury to all. And you are correct about that Brenner character. There's just something off about him. Something I can't put my finger on.'

'He's one scary sumbitch, I give him that much,' agreed Kenny.

Goins glared at his deputy. 'I ain't scared of no one, boy,' he said loudly. 'No one. Let alone some good for nothing high plains drifter. Tell you what we gonna do. Get Jonsey, Williams and Owens. Then you go to the armory and check out four Colt M4 carbines and two hundred rounds of ammunition. You all come and see me after and I'll tell you what we gonna do to the asshole that crippled your friend.'

Kenny smiled.

CHAPTER 10

The sheriff drove in through the front gates. Twelve foot of gold painted intricate iron scrollwork. Ornamental more than practical. They were gates that said, *look at me. I cost a lot of money. More money than you will ever have.* As opposed to gates that said, *fuck off. Go somewhere else.*

On the right-hand pillar next to the gate was a large brass sign. Deep engraved with black enamel script.

It read. 'Mount Olympus'.

The home of the gods.

Goins steered his Dodge Charger up the long curving driveway, the tires crunching on the crushed marble surface. The sun picked out the state motto painted on both of the front doors of the vehicle. *Salus Populi Suprema Lex Esto.* Let the welfare of the people be the supreme law.

He stopped in the parking area, walked up the stairs and entered the open front door without knocking. He was expected.

Mayor Henry Polk had servants. Many of them. But he didn't deem sheriff Goins of high enough stature to warrant sending his butler to greet him on his arrival.

Goins traversed the main corridor, knocked on the last door and entered the mayor's study.

Like the rest of the house it was an exercise in *nouvea riche* tastelessness. If it was metal, gold plate it, if it was glass, cut it into facets, if it was wood then polish it until it looked like a mirror.

The mayor was on speakerphone and he waved Goins to a seat.

'Well then, if you boys ain't big enough for those sorts of volumes then just tell me,' he said. 'Then I can go find me a distributor with bigger balls.'

'Now don't go talking like that,' crackled a voice from the speaker. 'After all, we have a deal.'

'So?' Asked Polk, the sneer obvious in his voice.

'You don't want to break a deal with us, buddy. Understand?'

'Are you threatening me?' Yelled Polk, his face going pale, 'Fuck you very much, Emile. Mayhap you just go get your gear someplace else. I own this fucking town and I tell you that I got more guns than you can even imagine. You come up here with that attitude and I swear to the lord that I will fuck you up so bad that your mama will fucking die from the sympathy pains, you piece of shit.'

'Hey, Hank. Settle down. We just negotiating here. Relax. Okay, we take more. Split the difference then. Be cool.'

Polk took a deep breath. 'Fine. Good. Give me three days to up my production. Three days from today you pick up. And don't fucking threaten me again.'

He disconnected the call.

'Fucking coonass thinks that he can threaten me. Dickwad.'

'Well you sure told him, Hank,' said Goins.

The mayor stared at the sheriff for a few seconds before he spoke. 'How many times I gotta tell you, Goins? You don't get to call me no Hank. I am, mayor or mister Polk. I am not your girlfriend so enough with the first names. Get it?'

Goins nodded. 'Sorry, mayor.'

'Whatever. Don't make a big deal of it. I called you up here to stress the importance of these next few days. Make sure that we are producing at top speed. This is a big deal, Goins. Big money. And I've pushed hard so we can't let these boys down.'

'You can rely on me, mayor.'

'Good. And when this motherfucker comes to collect, I want all the muscle that we have out on display. Everyone. A real show of force, like a fucking Soviet march-past. I want him to know who he's dealing with. Threaten me, will he? Asshole.'

***

Emile Beauchamp put his phone down and leaned back in his chair. 'Virgil.'

'Mister Beauchamp?'

'Get all the boys together, next three days time when we go up north we going to go in heavy handed. No one insults Emile Beauchamp that way. Red neck hillbilly piece of shit. We gonna take his drugs and burn his fucking town to the ground.'

Virgil smiled. All six foot seven and three hundred and eighty pounds of him. 'I do it now, sir'.

'*Ca c'est bon*, Virgil. Now go. Send Evangeline up. Oh, and the new girl... Genevieve, I think her name is. Why not? After all, I do own them.'

Virgil laughed and left to do his master's bidding.

CHAPTER 11

Brenner rode slowly. The engine was still knocking but at least he had a full tank of gas. He reflected on the fact that it had been the most expensive tank of gas that he had ever bought. He had contemplated arguing, but then he figured that it was a seller's market and simply paid up and left.

He saw Betty watching him through the window of the diner as he rode out, her expression hidden by the reflection off the glass. Every fiber of his being told him to turn around and go back. To put an end to whatever the hell was going on in that town. To make sure that the sheriff and his ilk paid for the way that they had treated Betty and her brother.

But then he remembered Betty's words.

Don't try to fix what ain't broke. I live a better life than most.

And who was he to disagree? Who was he to force his values on someone else?

A large truck barreled past him, the wind of its passing buffeting the bike. Heading for Goodbye. On its side a large red sign. 'Granger Industrial

Supplies. The world's largest manufacturer of Road Flares.'

'Weird,' murmured Brenner to himself. 'Why would anyone need so many road flares?'

He rode a while longer, noting the dappled light coming through the trees. The clear blueness of the sky above. The inherent peace of the place. The surrounding forest.

But as he rode he kept thinking. Slowing down as he did. Something at the back of his mind was trying hard to get noticed. Hard enough for him to concentrate less on where he was going and more on where he had been.

Road flares. Red Phosphorous.

And the drums at the chicken farm. Ammonia Hydroxide. Gallons of it.

'Shit,' he grunted as the dots joined up. 'The fuckers are making crystal meth.'

And by the quantities of the raw ingredients that he had seen, Brenner could extrapolate that they were manufacturing a shit-house full. Industrial quantities.

'Must be all of those mobile homes that I saw,' he said to himself. 'Clever. Split production. Split the risk.'

As he was about to turn his bike, the surrounding air was torn apart by the whiplash of scores of 5.56mm rounds. One hit the front tire, and another ricocheted off his gas tank. Then a round smashed into his shoulder, yet another struck his torso, low down on the right-hand side, exiting through his abdominals in a spray of blood. Two more rounds struck his right leg and another burned across his scalp, flooding his face with blood.

He opened the throttle on the Harley, fighting the flat tire to keep control as he powered through the ambush.

Then he ramped off the road and crashed into the forest. Leaving the bike where it landed, he limped away into the shadows, berating himself for a fool as he did so, struggling against the urge to black out.

CHAPTER 12

Betty watched the Ford F-250 pull into the parking area outside the sheriff's office. Four men climbed out. They seemed in high spirits, patting each other on the back and whooping like it was a snow day and they had gotten off school for the afternoon.

She knew them all. Deputies Kennedy, Owens, Jones and Williams. All four carried M4 carbines and wore Kevlar vests. Like they'd just come back from Iraq or something.

And her blood ran cold as they opened the tailgate of the load bed and pulled something off the back, dumping it on the grass in front of the entrance.

A matt black Harley Davidson. A 1962 pan head. And even from where she was she could see the bright scar on the side of the tank and the shredded tire. Bullet marks.

A tear rolled down her cheek. She had warned him. But it had been too late, Too late to save him.

'Why you sad?' Asked Boisy as he walked up to her, peering out at the scene that meant nothing to him.

Betty forced a smile. 'I'm not sad,' she lied.

'Then why are your eyes leaking?'

'It's the sun, Boisy. Just the sun. Now go and get the griddle ready for lunch, okay?'

Boisy nodded. 'I do good,' he said. 'Boisy make the griddle one hundred percent top notch extra fine for lunch.' He smiled. 'Then Betty-boo's eyes stop leaking and we all happy.'

Betty nodded and turned back to survey the events unfolding outside.

More cars were arriving. It looked like the sheriff had put the word out to all the deputies. As they arrived, they gathered around Brenner's bike and laughed and high-fived each other. Then the firemen arrived, walking over from the station, all of them of them.

Finally the sheriff came to the door and called everyone inside. Beckoning to them like he was inviting them to a matinee.

Betty hardened her heart and went to help Boisy prepare for lunch.

***

Every deputy apart from Richard Smelly sat in the briefing room. The air smelled of coffee and doughnuts and cheap aftershave. Goins stood at the front of the room, a smile on his face as he surveyed the twenty seven hard, well armed men. An army. Okay, a small army, he admitted to himself, but an army nonetheless.

'First things first, gentlemen,' he said. 'By now I am sure that you all heard about what happed to Richard.'

There was a general murmur of agreement expect for one deputy who raised his hand. 'Sorry, sheriff,' he said. 'I been at my Pa's the last few days, helping him with the mill. Just got back this morning.'

'Well, Jason,' said Goins. 'Richard got taken out by a drifter that came to town. Beat him real bad. Might even be permanent.'

'No,' exclaimed Jason. 'But Richard can't be taken out. He be the biggest toughest son bitch I know.'

'He sucker punched him,' interjected Kennedy. 'Attacked him from behind with a baseball bat or something. Fucking coward.'

'You arrest him?' Asked Jason.

'Better than that,' answered Kennedy. 'That's his bike outside.'

'And where is he?'

Kennedy laughed. 'Lying face down in the forest somewhere. We shot him up real good.'

There was a general cheering and Kennedy nodded his head. 'Yeah, you don't fuck with the Goodbye sheriff's department or else you get truly fucked up.'

'I got some more good news,' added Goins. 'Spoke to the doctor this morning and it looks like Richard is gonna pull through okay. Might be a slight limp is all.'

Everyone cheered again.

Goins held his hand up for silence. 'Right, boys,' he said. 'I want all hands on deck over the next couple of days. No leave, twenty-four shifts. The mayor has tasked us with quadrupling production for the next couple days. This is the big one, boys. We get this right and its bonuses all around. Proper fucking banker, city trader bonuses.'

Another round of cheers filled the room.

'Okay, men. Split into your usual teams, go to the warehouse at the chicken farm and draw inventory. I want you to make sure that all the cooks have enough stock of raw materials. Everything that they need to keep producing. No excuses.' He turned to the group of firemen. 'And you. I need you checking on everyone. Make sure that they're following the rules. No safety breaches. We don't need more explosions like that idiot Pinkerton caused. It's an unnecessary loss of stock, income and trained personal. So let's do it.'

With a final cheer the room emptied.

Goins stood alone for a while, a smile on his face.

Then he wiped the sweat from his brow with a large white handkerchief.

CHAPTER 13

The dark side of the moon.

No light. No air. No gravity.

Spinning. Coming back to earth.

Brenner's eyes snapped open, and he sucked air into his lungs like a drowning man.

'Hey, looky there. Wolf-boy be back with us.'

Brenner swiveled right. Mister Reeve and mister Bolin sat at the bar, shot glasses in their hands.

Brenner looked down. He was lying on an old army cot, naked. His wounds had been cleaned and he could see that they were almost healed. Deep, angry red pockmarks as opposed to massive gaping holes.

'How did I get here?'

'We brung you here. Weren't doing yourself no good lying out there in the forest bleedin' like that. No sir.'

'But, I was shot like miles away.'

Both of the old men cackled with laughter.

'Yep,' agreed mister Bolin. 'An you be a heavy so and so, I tell you. These old bones don't like carrying no shot up wolf-boy but sometime we gotta do what we gotta do.' He held out a full glass of clear liquid. 'Shine?'

Brenner stood up, walked over, accepted the offering and downed it in one. The rough spirits brought tears to his eyes and fire to his belly. He held out the glass for a refill and then went back to sitting on the edge of the cot.

'You got shot up pretty bad,' said mister Bolin. 'You were too weak to change, so we brung you back here and then we helped you to make the switch. Once you was in wolf form, then you healed up real quick.'

'Hallelujah,' added mister Reeve.

'Praise be,' agreed mister Bolin.

Brenner stared at the two old men, his golden eyes looking deeply, searching below the surface. 'Are you really here?'

They laughed. 'You know, you be pretty smart for a werewolf.'

'I'm not a werewolf,' denied Brenner. 'I'm a fucking failed genetic experiment.'

'Potato, poh-tah-toh,' observed mister Bolin.

Brenner leaned forward and grabbed mister Reeve's arm. 'Solid,' he said. 'So you are real?'

Mister Reeve shrugged. 'Maybe. Just because you can feel something don't necessarily mean that its real And likewise, vice versa. You can feel sunlight but you can't grasp it. You can grab water but you can't hold it in your fist. And even though they is both so will-o-wisp, they can both kill you.'

'My bike?'

Mister Bolin shook his head. 'Didn't see it. Not where you was at any rate.'

'So who shot you up boy?' Asked mister Reeve.

'I can only guess. Most likely those fucking hillbilly deputies from Goodbye.'

'So what you do now?'

'Now? I go back and make them wish that they had killed me,' growled Brenner.

'Careful, boy,' said mister Bolin. 'Vengeance is mine sayeth the Lord.'

'Not while I'm around,' said Brenner. 'When I'm around then vengeance is mine. And it is swift and it is abso-fucking-lute.'

CHAPTER 14

Mama Acadia had chalked out the pentagram and evoked the powers of air, earth, fire and water. Then she had called on the relevant gods, Elohim, El, Adonaj and Nanta.

Finally she had sacrificed the cockerel, slashing its throat and sprinkling the blood over all the points of the pentagram. Then she fell to the floor as her Loa mounted her.

Twenty minutes later she came too. She had bitten her lips and tongue and cut her head on the floor. Her body ached from the strain of muscle cramp and she was covered in deep bruises.

As she struggled to her feet, she knew that something was badly wrong. Her Loa, Ayizan, normally mounted her quietly and with dignity. But this time he had done so with undue haste and no small amount of fear.

And for a Loa to feel fear she knew that much was wrong.

Nevertheless, he had passed on his messages and now she had to talk to her benefactor, **Emile Beauchamp**.

Moving slowly so as to favor her injuries, Mama Acadia walked up the stairs from the basement to the entrance hall on the first floor of the Creole Townhouse situated in the French Quarter of New Orleans.

The hall was larger than most as Emile had purchased the townhouses on both sides and knocked through, creating a series of huge reception areas for the well-known parties that he habitually threw. In the corner stood a grand piano, on the polished hardwood floors a series of loom-woven Cajun rag rugs. The walls glowed with subtly lit art and indoor plants gave the entire area a feeling of calm and seclusion.

A feeling that totally belied the personality of the man who owned the house.

Emile Beauchamp had grown up in the bayou from a young black mother and an absent French-Canadian father. He had seven siblings, all girls. With no formal schooling, Emile had supplemented the family income from the age of five by digging for red worms and selling them to the fishermen on the bayou. By the time he was eight he had expanded his stock to include alcohol and tobacco. By his thirteenth birthday he could also supply women. Or even young men if the need so arose.

While not a large man, Emile learned early on that physical power could be cheaply purchased. It was mental capacity that separated the leaders from the peons. The first muscle that he had hired were the identical twins, the Delaroche brothers. They were only sixteen years old at the time and larger than any other human beings that Emile had previously come across.

Now, twenty years on, Virgil and Henri both stood exactly six foot seven in their socks and weighed in at a matching three hundred and sixty pounds of muscle and sinew and bone. A combined total of over seven hundred pounds of pissed off.

And they were fanatically loyal to Emile Beauchamp.

Aside from them, Emile claimed another seventeen men, all of Cajun extraction, all loyal to the point of fanaticism and all of circus freak dimensions. Emile liked his muscle big and bad.

Mama Acadia continued up the stairs to the first floor and went straight to Emile's study. Virgil blocked her way, putting out a hand the size of a large ham. Mama slapped it with her fan. 'Get out my face, you gorilla,' she snapped. 'Me got big news for the man.'

'He don't want be disturbed, Mama,' rumbled Virgil, his hand still in front of the door.

'I don't care. Now you step aside or Mama gonna make things uncomfortable for you, Virgil.'

The huge man scowled and then stepped aside. He was loyal, but he wasn't stupid. And no one stood in Mama Acadia's way on purpose. Not unless you wanted to spend the rest of your days wondering around like a brainless fool. A zombie in her thrall. Or so went the rumors.

Mama stormed in.

Emile was on the phone and he waved Mama to a seat. But after seeing her expression he excused himself from the caller and replaced the receiver.

'What wrong, Mama?'

'I been communing with Ayizan.'

'Your Loa?'

'The same.'

'What he got to say?'

Mama shook her head. 'He be awful perturbed. Normal he ride me like a saint but this time he treated me like a five and dime street whore. Done bash me about like an unloved step child.'

Emile stood up, walked over to a liquor table and poured brandy in to two crystal balloons. He handed one to Mama who took it thankfully, even though it wasn't yet ten o'clock in the morning.

They toasted each other.

'Talk to me, Mama.'

'This deal you doing with the hillbilly. The Ozark mountain boys. It smells bad.'

'In what way?'

'There be trouble there, Emile. With a capital T.'

Emile laughed. 'Yeah, I know. The chief hillbilly threatened me this morning. There be nothing to worry about, Mama. He just hot air and piss. Them redneck motherfuckers won't get nothing over Beauchamp.'

'It's not him,' said Mama.

'Who then?'

'I don't know, my child. But I see strength. Power. Moonlight. A terrible enemy.'

'I take care of whoever that is. No man can stand against me.'

'There is more. Another one. Darkness. Death himself walking the earth. Evil He seeks the first one.' Mama's eyes rolled back in her head, reveling two white orbs. 'Evil,' she shrieked. And then she started to weep. 'Please don't go, Emile,' she begged. 'Send your men but you stay here.'

Emile took a deep breath. He didn't take Mama Acadia's warnings lightly. She had been with him for many years now and although her advice was often cryptic, it was never wrong.

'I have to go, Mama,' he said. 'Or else those redneck motherfuckers done think that Emile just some poor New Orleans oyster boy with no balls nor brains. In fact me and the boys are leaving first thing tomorrow. It be a long trip. Don't you worry none. Beauchamp he be the baddest mother around.'

'You don't understand, my darling child,' whispered Mama. 'The watchers are there as well.'

'The watchers? Are they dangerous?'

Mama shook her head. 'Not really. They just be two irritating old men. They can't do nothing. But the fact is, if they there then bad things are going to happen. It's what they do. They wait and they watch. And they haven't deemed anything worth watching for a very long time now. So them being there is no good thing. Don't go.'

Emile smiled, his teeth white against his dark skin. 'Old men and unknown evil Mama? None of that matters. Remember, even though I walk through the shadow of the valley of death I shall fear no evil, for I be the baddest son of a bitch in the valley. And don't you forget that.' He leaned over and kissed Mama on the forehead. 'Now I gots to go and see some folk. You stay here, finish up your brandy and relax. And don't forget, Emile Beauchamp be the baddest man in town.'

He winked and left.

Mama shook her head as slow, fat tears ran down her cheeks. 'Not this time, my son,' she whispered to herself. 'Not this time.'

CHAPTER 15

Every town, no matter how upmarket, has to have its dark side. A place for the bottom feeders to dwell. A place where drugs are dealt, bodies are sold and deals are made. A place where the seedier side of humanity is allowed out of its cage and into the open.

No star motels and hotels that rented rooms by the hour. Streets with broken street lamps and walls covered in graffiti.

This was where Brenner often lived. Off the grid off the radar and out of sight.

So that it where sergeant Solomon Hopewell went to find him.

He walked into the reception area of the motel and showed the man at the desk the photo.

He stared blankly at Solomon and then spat into a tin on the desk. A stream of brown tobacco juice. A little dribbled down his chin, and he made no attempt to wipe it off.

Solomon placed a fifty dollar bill on the desk, deciding to try honey instead of the stick for a change.

The tobacco chewer sneered at the bill. 'I'm no fucking street whore, mister. You wanna fuck me you put down some meaningful cash.'

The sergeant sighed and shook his head. 'You know, what happened to civility and good manners?' He said. 'Was a day when fifty dollars could prevent a little violence. Buy some information and maybe even a little respect. A thank you, for example. And now it gets a sneer from a piece of shit who needs a bath, in charge of a piece of shit establishment, chewing on shitty tobacco while wearing a shitty nylon lounge shirt.'

'Hey, fuck you,' said the receptionist in a truly offended voice. 'This isn't a nylon shirt. It's a viscose-cotton blend.'

'Whatever,' shrugged Solomon as he held up the photo again. 'Seen this man?'

The man turned away.

Solomon's right hand snapped out in a blur of movement as he grabbed the man's ear and, with a simple twist of his wrist, tore it off.

The man screamed out aloud as he clutched at his head, trying unsuccessfully to stem the flow of blood. 'Jesus, dude,' he shouted. 'You pulled my bloody ear off, you psycho.'

Solomon shook his head. 'Tut, tut. How inconvenient for you.' He held up the photo again. 'Seen him?'

'Yes. Yes, you fucking nutcase. I seen him two days ago. Took a room, paid cash. Didn't talk, rode a black rat bike. Harley I think. Jesus.' He scrabbled around on the desk. 'Where's my fucking ear?'

Solomon tossed it onto the desk. 'There. Put it on ice. Sometimes they can sew them back on. Probably not that one though,' he observed. 'That one's pretty fucked up.' Then he leaned over the desk and punched the man. A solid blow that shattered his nose and dropped him to the floor, unconscious. 'That's for being rude. And I don't care what your shirt's made of, it's shitty.'

Solomon walked back to his car. As he got there, the driver opened his door for him. At the same time, another man approached. He wore a light colored suit, crocodile skin boots, blond hair and a baseball cap.

'Hey, high roller,' he said 'You looking for some action? I got chemicals; I got girls I got boys.'

'Well, unless you got a death wish, I suggest that you fuck off,' warned Solomon, eager to get moving.

'Hey homes, don't be like that.'

'Listen, homes. You must be one of the whitest boys I ever did meet. So don't try to get all street on me. Now I've been polite. Fuck off.'

There was the unmistakable sound of a switchblade being flicked open.

Solomon rolled his eyes. 'Is it just me,' he said to no one in particular. 'Or have the youth of today gotten stupider?'

His driver shrugged. 'I blame MTV sir. Texting, Facebook. Instant gratification. No attention span.'

Brenner nodded. 'You're probably correct.'

The pimp lunged at Solomon who didn't even bother to move. The knife struck him in the chest and the pimp stepped back, leaving the blade protruding.

Solomon raised an eyebrow and smiled.

The pimp went pale and he let out an involuntary squeak of fear.

'You know,' said the sergeant. 'I reckon that its right about now that your hind brain has finally caught up with your inherent stupidity,' he said.

The dude stared at Solomon in disbelief. 'What the fuck?'

'Exactly,' agreed Solomon as he pulled the knife out and smacked it into the pimp's right eye, dropping him like a stone. 'Most definitely, what the fuck.'

Solomon shook his head as he got into the car. 'No class, that's the real problem,' he said. 'No class.'

'I agree,' said his driver.

Solomon took out a cell phone and dialed. 'Colonel. We are getting closer. I'll call again when I have more solid news.'

He disconnected the call. Then he opened his briefcase, selected a syringe and exposed the needle.

His elixir.

His life's blood.

His bane.

He thrust it deep into his neck.

CHAPTER 16

Brenner ran through the forest. Alpha. Huge. A wolf the size of a horse. Absolutely silent. Like a spirit animal as opposed to something made from flesh and blood.

He reveled in the crisp air, the smell of pine and ozone, the sound of small game scattering before him.

Bursting through a thicket he saw in front of him, three timber wolves. A male and two females. He stopped immediately, surprised to see them so far east. All of them lay down instantly and exposed their throats and bellies to him, tongues lolling from the sides of their mouths in a show of subservience. He sniffed at them and then left, continuing on towards the town of Goodbye.

After a while he turned to see that they were following him, keeping pace as they ran softly behind him.

Brenner growled at them. *Go. Danger.*

They hesitated but then continued to follow.

Brenner growled again. *No. Bad men. Danger.*

The male whined back. *You leader. Must help.*

Pack.

Brenner shook his head. *Not pack. Lone wolf. Leave.*

When he set off again the wolves stayed, their expressions obedient but baffled.

The alpha wolf ran on alone again. Brenner didn't have a plan. He had been aggrieved. They had tried to kill him so he sought retribution.

But as well as that he knew that there were wrongs that needed to be righted. As a rule, Brenner couldn't give a goddam about drugs or drug users. He was basically a child of the sixties and had personally tried most recreational drugs at some time or another.

But meth was bad. Any hard core drug that you could mix up in a home kitchen didn't bode well.

And also, they were assholes.

His wolf form ate up the miles and soon he could see the chicken farm. The sun was sinking below the horizon but there was still a hive of happenings going on.

Floodlights were on, bathing the area in an electric blue-white glare and pickup trucks were lined up outside the warehouse. Forklifts were loading barrels and cases onto the trucks.

Brenner picked out one of the loaded trucks that was heading away from the farm and followed it, easily keeping up as it bounced down the rutted tracks that headed past the town. He continued following it through the surrounding forest all the way to a trailer home.

The driver and passenger got out of the pickup to be met by a group of three people. Two men and a girl. There was a brief greeting, a hand shake and then they all unloaded some of the crates and barrels from the back of the vehicle, carrying it into the trailer home.

When the pickup left Brenner followed it once again. It stopped at another trailer home and similar quantity of goods were unloaded.

Then on to yet another trailer, after which the load area of the pickup was empty, and the vehicle headed back towards the chicken farm.

Brenner ran alongside it for a while, making sure that he remained unseen, keeping to the shadows. And when they got to a particularly secluded part of the forest, Brenner cut hard right and slammed into the truck, shouldering it off the road and onto a tree.

The windscreen shattered, and the radiator blew with an explosion of steam. The driver stayed slumped over the steering wheel but the passenger got out, wielding a pump action shotgun. Brenner ripped the weapon out of the man's hands, grabbing the barrel with his huge jaws and flicking it into the forest. Then he pushed the man to the ground and held him there with one massive paw.

While the man was pinned down, Brenner checked out the driver. He was still slumped over the steering wheel and Brenner could see that he wouldn't be moving soon, courtesy of a deep head wound that was bleeding copiously. In fact Brenner guessed that the man would bleed to death of he didn't get some serious help mighty quickly. And there was little chance of that happening.

So, knowing he had time, Brenner changed into his Wolfman form so that he could communicate. As he did so he smelled the acrid odor of urine and, glancing down he saw that his captive had literally pissed his pants in terror, a dark stain spreading down the front of his trousers.

'Really?' Growled Brenner. 'Don't you got no control?'

The man whimpered, his teeth clicking together like he was suffering from hyperthermia.

'How many trailers are there?' Asked The Wolfman.

'Not sure,' stammered the urine soaked man.

'Think,' growled Brenner. 'Your life may very well depend on this.'

'I think about fifty,' answered the man. 'There's a map in the truck. The compartment in the driver's door.' Tears started to run down the man's face as the shock and horror that he was feeling, ate away at his masculinity.

The Wolfman grabbed the door handle and pulled, tearing off the entire door by mistake. He held it in his hand for a few seconds and then shook his head as he dropped it. 'Oops.' He changed to full human so that he could get the map from the cab.

As he did, he heard the click of the safety behind him. Morphing instantly and throwing himself to one side as urine stain fired, he avoided the slug. Then, springing forward, he grabbed the man's head in one huge clawed hand and squeezing hard as he did so. The man's cranium crunched like a hard candy in a dogs jaws and his body went limp. Brenner shook him around a little, like the world's biggest terrier attacking a human sized rat, and then he dropped the lifeless body to the floor and ran off, the map still clutched in his claws.

CHAPTER 17

Brenner arrived back at the first trailer that the pickup had visited. The two men and the woman were inside. He could hear them talking. Arguing over something. Nothing serious, merely simple meaningless domestic type disagreements.

He squatted down outside the structure to think. He had to make a decision on how escalate the situation. These were drug dealers. But only in a peripheral way. Cooks, not distributors. Did that warrant a death penalty? And even if it did, who was he to pass sentence?

He made his decision and, remaining in Wolfman form he walked up to the trailer and knocked on the front door, his superhuman strength almost bashing it off its hinges as he did so.

One of the men whipped the door open.

'Hey, what the fuck?' He shouted.

Brenner grabbed his shirtfront and casually tossed him thirty feet into a tree. Then he tried to get inside the home but couldn't fit through the narrow front door. He growled in frustration and started to rip away the door jamb.

Inside the woman started to scream frantically, rooted to the spot by fear. Brenner saw the other male attempting to escape via a window at the back of the house so he extricated himself from the ruined doorway and sprinted around, grabbing the escapee as he was halfway out of the window. Dragging the man around to the front of the house he pointed at the girl.

'Get her out,' he growled, his massive lupine jaw and teeth chopping and grinding the words up as he spoke. A savage facsimile of human speech.

The man shook with fear. 'What?' He asked. 'I can't… what?'

Brenner concentrated, forming the words slower and with more care. 'Get. The. Girl.'

The man ran into the house, grabbed the woman's arm, hauled her out and deposited her on the ground in front of the Wolfman.

Brenner gazed down at the two of him, his golden eyes like twin headlights. 'Run.'

They ran, stumbling and falling in their haste to get away.

And behind them, Brenner hunched his shoulders, grabbed the underside of the trailer home and with a massive surge of strength flipped it on its side, spinning it in the air when he did so.

As the trailer took off, he was already running for cover.

Seconds later a massive fireball lit up the night.

The cook and the girl peered into the darkness but the Wolfman was gone. Both of them sank to the floor. Their eyes full of fear. Full of the realization that the monsters under the bed were real after all.

***

Brenner's claw marked the spot, punching through the map. He ran a bit further and then came upon the next trailer home. Outside there was a junkyard dog. A pit-bull with a scarred face and a chewed up ear. It took one look at Brenner and rolled over onto his back.

The Wolfman rubbed its tummy, and it wagged its tail.

Then Brenner walked over to the window and looked inside. A single male. Dressed in a button down white shirt and a college jersey. The place looked neat. His apparatus clean. Almost like a school science project.

Brenner looked at the dog. *Bark,* he commanded.

The pit-bull stood up and started to bark like his life depended on it.

'Shut up, Tyson,' shouted the preppie look-alike from the trailer.

Tyson continued barking, doubling the volume.

The door banged open and the meth-cook stepped outside, in his right hand a leather riding crop. He walked over to the chained up dog and raised his whip-hand high. 'Time for some discipline, you stupid mutt.'

As he brought his hand down Brenner stepped forward, appearing out of the shadows like a wraith. He grasped the man's wrist, his hand a steel trap.

The dog beater turned to look into the eyes of the seven foot monster that seemed to have appeared as if by magic and his whole body went limp. 'Oh, shit,' he whispered.

Brenner nodded. 'Very, oh shit,' he agreed. Then he turned to Tyson. 'Hey, dog. You want some?'

Tyson growled and Brenner forced the meth-cook down to his knees next to the abused pit-bull. 'There you go, dude,' he said to Tyson. 'Knock yourself out.'

The pit-bull launched itself at his ex-master, jaws open wide,

Brenner walked over to the trailer, grunted, heaved.

Seconds later the sky was lit up by another fireball.

As the Wolfman left, he snapped the chain keeping Tyson imprisoned. The dog wagged its tail and licked Brenner's leg, his maw still covered in blood.

Brenner winked and was gone.

CHAPTER 18

'What the living hell is going on?' Shouted sheriff Goins at the top of his voice, his face puce from the effort. As if, somehow, mere volume could replace intel and would help get to the bottom of things. 'It looks like a fucking air raid going on out there.' He grabbed Kennedy by the arm. 'Get some men out into the forest. Take a couple of firemen with you. Find out what's happening and stop it. Now. That's money burning up out there. Our money.'

As he was shouting another explosion lit up the night sky, the soft thump and following rumble shivering across them like the coming of a great storm.

His cell phone rang, and he answered it. 'Mayor? Yes, sir. No idea, sir, but I am on it. I'll phone you back as soon as we know anything.' He disconnected the call. 'Asshole,' he screamed at the phone in frustration.

CHAPTER 19

They called him, Fingerless. Not that he had no fingers, in fact he had only lost one. His ring finger on his right hand. He had caught it in a potato picking machine when he was a little kid and, kids being kids, the nickname of Fingerless had stuck right through to adulthood.

Fingerless took a drag of his cigarette, unzipped his jeans and started to pee, humming to himself as he did so.

Behind him he could hear the other men laughing and joking while they played cards. They better not have started a hand without him, thought Fingerless as he tried to rush the flow so that he could get back to the table.

That's when he saw the shadow in the forest. Huge and hulking. Impossibly human-like but quite obviously some sort of animal. Far too large and fast to be human. Eschewing his normal flick-dry routine he crammed himself back into his jeans before he'd quite finished and ran for the trailer, kicking the door open and talking before he had stopped running.

'Bear,' he shouted.

The five men in the trailer all turned as one to look at him. Four sat around the table playing poker. Real poker, five card draw. The fifth was at the stove cooking meth. In the corner of the room, stacked against the wall stood five rifles and a shotgun.

'Hey, I just saw a bear outside,' repeated Fingerless. 'Or a mountain lion. Maybe. I dunno, but something real big.'

'Bullshit,' retorted Ted, the leader of the group. Big man, wide, black bearded, small eyed and meaner than a snake.

'No bullshit, Ted. A huge fucking bear. Or lion. Maybe a wolf. Look it's dark out there but I saw something.'

'So?'

'So, let's shoot it.'

The men all cheered, dropped their cards, grabbed the rifles and piled out of the cabin. The cook took the shotgun and picked up a huge, military grade, hand held searchlight. He turned it on and scanned the forest. They saw a brief shadow. Almost nothing. A mere darker patch amongst the darkness.

But it was enough. Amped up and ready to go they all opened fire at once.

Brenner dropped to the ground to avoid the fusillade of shots that cracked and whined about him. He grinned to himself. *Man, that was close. Damn hillbillies are quick on the draw.*

Moving faster than a man could run, he crawled forward and went around the back of the trailer, avoiding the men all clustered at the front. As soon as he arrived at his destination, he sprang up onto the roof and howled.

The men all tuned and stared at him, their faces registering their shock.

Then he jumped into them. He didn't hold back, figuring that anyone who shot at him was fair game. If you try to kill me, I might just do the same to you. After all, fair is fair.

Smashing left and right Brenner removed firearms, broke limbs and tore flesh. Then one of the men drew a Glock pistol. Brenner reacted without thinking, slashing at the man's neck he sliced through his vertebrae, separating the head from the body and sending it flying off into the trees.

The headless body dropped to the ground, the pistol still clutched tightly in its right hand.

Brenner shook his head. He hadn't really wanted to kill any of the men, but then that one shouldn't have drawn down on him. He checked that the others were all incapacitated, picked up the weapons and headed for the trailer, changing to human form as he did so in order to be able to fit through the door.

Once in, he dumped the rifles and shotgun on the floor and then checked that all the chemicals weren't next to the stove and the caps were on all the bottles. Then he scouted around, going through a few drawers. He soon found a rucksack.

A few boxes of ammunition. He helped himself to twenty rounds of 308 match grade ammo and paired it with one of the rifles. A Les Baer semi-auto with a twenty round magazine. He nodded appreciatively. Custom weapon. Not cheap. *These meth heads make too much money.* He thought. 'Talking about money,' he said to himself as he checked some of the more usual hiding places. Finally he found a wad of cash in the freezer. 'Original,' he laughed.

Brenner did a quick count. Twenty grand in hundreds. He put the cash in the haversack. Then he looked for some clothes but they were all too small. Finally he settled on T-shirt and a clean pair of boxers, reckoning they should fit at a stretch and were better than nothing at all.

Brenner collected all the red phosphorus that the cooker had already separated from the road flares. He mixed it with ethyl alcohol and kneaded it into a stiff paste. Then he carefully warmed it in a pan until it was almost completely dry.

Grabbing a few glass jars he filled five of them with the mix, screwed the tops on tight and then punching a hole in them with a knife and inserted the striking mechanism from a road flare. Finally he bound each jar in layers and layers of duct tape.

He placed four of the homemade phosphorus bombs into the rucksack, strapped the rifle to it and carried it outside, placing it a hundred yards away before morphing into Wolfman mode. Taking the fifth homemade bomb, Brenner struck the ignition and threw it. His Wolfman enhanced strength sent the jar like a bullet and it smashed through the trailer window as the flare ignited the explosive.

Brenner was impressed. The entire trailer lifted twenty feet into the air as the bomb went off. Burning pieces of phosphorous scattered through the night sky like an explosion of stars. A massive cloud of white smoke billowed up, catching the light of the gibbous moon that turned it blue.

Brenner nodded in satisfaction, Time to go to the source. He growled as he started to run.

It took him less than half an hour to reach the warehouse in the chicken farm and as soon as he got there he simply ran up to the complex and threw a bomb in.

Seconds later the vast stores of ethyl alcohol, ammonia and road flares exploded like Mount Vesuvius erupting.

Miraculously, none of the chickens were harmed.

Brenner grinned and headed for town.

It was time to up the ante.

CHAPTER 20

Emile Beauchamp and his retinue were driving in convoy from New Orleans to Goodnight. Three luxury limousines, eleven well armed, big men. It would normally be a twelve hour drive but Emile had decided to bunk over in Memphis for the night. Home of the blues.

He had an accounting problem with one of his retailers and felt the need to apply a generous amount of discipline.

He and his posse were staying at the River Inn overlooking the Mississippi River. A five star boutique hotel that suited Emile's sense of style and grace. But before they could check in there he had decided to head straight for a somewhat less salubrious part of town.

The Shelby Forest area.

They parked outside a normal looking two story house in a normal looking residential street in the neighborhood. The area was decidedly down-market. No fences, lawns like a dog's mange, discarded paper bags and random pieces of rusting steel adorned the gardens. On the power lines above hung at least fifty pairs of trainers, tied together with their own shoelaces and thrown over the lines.

Installation art.

Emile sneered. 'Why for this man live like this? I know he be making a small fortune. And that be before he started stealing from me.'

Virgil shrugged. 'Some people are only happy surrounded by others just like them. The man don't wanna raise himself above the shit, he just wanna be the biggest piece of shit in the crapper. Man got no style.'

Emile laughed. 'Truth you speak, Virgil. He not like us.'

Both Virgil and Henri nodded. 'Not like us, boss.'

'Come on,' said Emile. 'We go in. Tell the rest of the boys to stay out here. Watch the cars and watch our back. Tell them we don't wanna be disturbed.'

Virgil did the rounds and came back in under a minute.

'Let's go then boys,' said Emile. He gestured to the door. 'Henri. Knock. Firmly.'

Henri smiled, closed his fist and punched the door so hard that it flew off its hinges and into the corridor.

Emile nodded. 'Thank you, Henri.'

Henri went in first, followed by Emile with Virgil bringing up the rear. They went down the corridor and into a sitting room. As they got to the door, two men rushed out, looking for what was happening. Bristling with aggression.

Henri simply cuffed them both on the side of their heads as they ran out, slamming them against the doorjamb and rendering them unconscious.

There were three more men and three women sitting in the lounge. Red overstuffed leather furniture, lava lamps, blue shaggy pile carpet. On the wall, a massive seventy five inch TV, blasting out rap music. A DVD of Scoolboy Q.

Emile drew his Colt 45 and emptied the entire seven round magazine into the screen. 'I fucking hate rap,' he said. 'Why can't you play some decent music. Michael Buble or Neil Diamond?'

No one answered.

'I'm talking to you, Desharious. You can fucking tell because I'm looking at you and my lips are moving.' Emile handed the empty pistol to Virgil who ejected the empty mag, slapped in a full one, and handed it back.

'You shot my TV,' said Desharious in amazement. 'That was brand new.'

'Had to,' replied Emile. 'Fucking stupid noise was making my teeth itch. Anyway, tell me, motherfucker, why you been stealing from me?'

Desharious shook his head vehemently. Side to side like a bobble head dog. Or a toddler lying to his mum. 'No way, mister Beauchamp. I wouldn't dare.'

'Yes you would dare,' contradicted Emile. 'Because you did.'

Suddenly one of the girls started to scream in delayed reaction to the gunfire.

Emile flinched at the high pitched sound. 'Seriously? What the fuck is her problem?'

'I dunno, mister Beauchamp,' answered Desharious. 'Bad trip, I reckon.'

'Tell the bitch to shut up.'

Desharious turned to the girl and patted her arm. 'Hey Shaniquwa. Calm down, baby. Stop screaming.'

The girl paid no attention to Desharious' request and, if anything, both the pitch and the volume increased.

Emile raised his 45 and shot her in the face. Her head whipped back in a spray of blood and she fell to the floor.

'Ah,' said Emile. 'Blessed silence. Now, as I was saying, Desharious.' Emile paused, a thoughtful look on his face. 'Desharious? That your real name?'

The drug dealer nodded.

'It be a stupid name. From now on I'm going to call you, Frank. Happy?'

Desharious didn't answer.

'Now, Frank,' continued Emile. 'Why you steal from me.'

'Didn't, mister Beauchamp.'

'You did.'

'Didn't.'

'Did.'

'Didn't.'

'Oh for fuck sake,' shouted Emile, as he shot the

man who used to be called Desharious in the chest. Then he stood up and walked out of the room. 'Kill the rest of them,' he commanded Virgil as he left. 'Make it messy. I want people to know that you don't fuck with Beauchamp.'

CHAPTER 21

Most of the trailers on the map were burning and Brenner was heading back to town, ostensibly to check up on Betty and Boisy. To see if they were okay.

He ghosted down the street, past the diner and around the back. Then he stood in the shadows outside the back door to listen for them.

As he stopped, however, Betty opened the back door to take out the trash and saw him standing there in full Wolfman mode.

Her hand flew to her mouth, and she was about to scream when Boisy walked out, took one look and waved.

'Hello, mister Brenner,' he said. 'The diner's closed but I can cook you something here. You want something to eat? Boisy make you some steak. Nice steak. You hungry mister Brenner?'

The Wolfman tilted his head to one side and then he nodded.

Boisy smiled and went back inside, taking out pans and readying his ingredients.

Betty stood still, her face a picture of amazement.

'Brenner?'

He nodded and, at the same time, he changed back into human form.

Boisy laughed from the kitchen. 'Hey mister Brenner,' he said. 'You forgot to put your clothes on.'

Brenner smiled. 'So I did, Boisy,' he said as he opened the rucksack and pulled on the boxers and the t-shirt that he had appropriated. They were both so tight as to make almost no difference to his previous nakedness.

Betty laughed.

Brenner shrugged. 'It's all that I could find. And I reckoned that it was better than nothing.'

'Well it isn't,' said Betty. 'Come on in, I've got some clothes upstairs. They used to belong to our daddy. He was a big man. They should fit as long as you don't mind looking like a lumberjack.'

Five minutes later, Brenner was sitting at the kitchen table dressed in faded jeans, a checked blanket shirt, leather braces and steel toe working boots.

Boisy placed a plateful of blood-rare steaks in front of him.

Betty scowled. 'Boisy,' she said. 'Those aren't hardly even warmed up.'

Her brother nodded. 'Mister Brenner wants them like that,' he insisted. 'When he forgets his clothes he wants his meat raw.'

Brenner raised an eyebrow. 'He's right,' he confirmed. 'Not sure how he knows, but he's bang on the money.'

'What the hell is going on, Brenner?' Asked Betty. 'What are you? I thought that you were dead. What are you doing out there?'

'What am I,' repeated Brenner. 'I'm a freak. I'm a failed military experiment. Many years ago, back in Vietnam, the military did some work on me. As well as a bunch of other grunts. Long story short, at the end of it I was what you see sitting here. Half man, half wolf. Every full moon I change and lose control. I ran away and they're still hunting me. Look,' said Brenner. 'I'm sorry. I'm trying to compress a fifty year story into a few sentences, so it probably doesn't make a lot of sense.'

'You're a werewolf,' said Betty.

'No,' denied Brenner. 'I'm a genetic experiment.'

'Occam's Razor,' mumbled Boisy.

Brenner raised an eyebrow.

'What's Boisy talking about?' Asked Betty. 'What's an okam razor?'

'Occam's Razor,' corrected Brenner. 'Also known as the Law of Parsimony. Attributed to a Franciscan friar called Occam. He said, *Among competing hypotheses, the one with the fewest assumptions should be selected.*'

'In other words,' said Betty. 'If it looks like a duck, swims like a duck, and quacks like a duck, then it probably is a duck.'

'I suppose so,' admitted Brenner.

'So, you're a werewolf.'

Brenner shook his head. Then he turned to Boisy.

'How did you know about Occam's Razor, Boisy?'

The boy shrugged. 'Boisy good cook. You want more food, mister Brenner?'

'No thanks, Boisy,' answered Brenner. 'That was great, thank you very much.'

'Keep talking, Wolfman,' said Betty. 'How come you aren't dead? They brought your bike back, and it looked like it had been shot up. Then they was all like high-fiving and acting like general shit heads. I thought that you were dead for sure.'

Brenner nodded. 'Yep, they bushwhacked me. Bunch of them shot me up real good. I was lucky I survived.'

'You look fine now.'

'Fast healer.'

'And all these explosions?' Continued Betty. 'The fires.'

'Payback.'

Betty shook her head. 'You got a death wish, Brenner,' she said. 'Okay, you been lucky so far. But there's an army of deputies out there. And they are well armed and well motivated. You can't beat them all. There are simply too many of them.'

'Well, by this time tomorrow there gonna be a whole lot less of them,' answered Brenner. 'Like, none at all.'

'And then?'

'And then nothing. You don't grab a wolf by the tail and expect nothing to happen. Bunch of drug dealers, murderers and rapists.'

'So you have decided to be the judge and the jury.'

'No. I am wrath. I am vengeance.'

'Brenner, these are real bad people.'

'I am what happens to bad people,' said Brenner as he stood up. 'Thanks again for the chow, Boisy. You a good cook.'

Boisy nodded. 'Be careful mister Brenner.'

Brenner opened the door and faded into the night.

CHAPTER 22

'What the fuck is going on down there?' Shouted mayor Polk into his cell phone. 'It looks like Iraq from up here. Everything is burning. Everything.'

'I honestly do not know, mayor,' answered sheriff Goins. 'I got the boys out searching but no joy yet. Don't worry, give us a little time and we'll get them, whoever they are.'

'It's that fucking Cajun coonass and his boys,' yelled Polk. 'They're trying to take over our operation.'

'With all due respect, mayor. That makes no sense. If they wanted to take over why would they start by blowing everything to hell in a hand-basket? Although I must admit, whoever it is hasn't actually killed many of the cooks. Just laid them out.'

See,' said the mayor. 'That's because they want to keep the means of production alive. Shit. Sheriff, send some boys up here. At least ten of them. That son bitch is gonna come for me, I can feel it in my bones'.

'I'll send a few deputies up there to protect you,

mayor.'

'Not a few, dickwad,' shouted Polk. 'Lots. All that you can spare. Remember who butters your bread, sheriff.'

'Straight away, mayor.' Goins disconnected. 'Asswipe,' he mumbled to himself. 'Hey, Kennedy. Find five deputies and send them up to mayor Polk's house. Make sure they're well armed. The old man is shitting himself. Needs babysitting.'

'Right on sheriff,' affirmed Kennedy as he ran off.

Goins scrubbed his face with his hands. 'Who the hell is doing this? And how many of them are there? Why haven't we seen anyone?' He kicked his car door. 'Shit, shit, shit, shitshitshit!'

***

Brenner walked down the main street. Out in the open. Human. Dressed in Betty's father's lumberjack shirt, jeans and boots. Over his shoulder the rucksack and rifle. As he walked past the sheriff's office, he noticed that the lights were on and there were at least fifteen people inside. Only two deputies, the rest being office workers.

He kept going until he reached the fire station. Sticking to the shadows, he checked the place out. No one there. Both the tankers were gone but the ladder truck was still parked in its bay.

Brenner shrugged off the rucksack, took out one of the phosphorus bombs, ripped the igniter and tossed it into the station, under the fire truck.

Then he calmly walked away.

Ten seconds later there was a massive explosion.

Brenner watched from the shadows as everyone ran out of the sheriff's office and into the street, gawping at the burning fire station.

He quickly scanned the sheriffs' building. Empty. So he chucked a bomb through the front window, deep into the building. Followed quickly by a second.

The resulting explosion lifted the roof off. Flames billowed out into the sky with a rolling ball of fire. Seconds later the armory began to cook and thousands of rounds of ammunition start exploding.

The crowd in the street went mental. Running around like headless chickens. Residents ran out of their houses to see what was happening, pointing and gesticulating like mine artists on speed. Some people simply sat down, shaking their heads like it was simply too much to take in.

Others shouted unnecessary orders and advice to no one in particular.

'Phone the fire department.'

'The fire departments on fire, you dick.'

'Well phone the sheriff's department.'

'The sheriff's departments also on fire, you dick.'

'Well fuck you.'

'Fuck you.'

Fist fights start breaking out as panic turned to aggression.

Brenner looked for the two deputies on the crowd. They were the enemy. Everything else was collateral damage. They may or may not be the men that shot him but that didn't matter. They were of the same brotherhood. The same pack.

They have been marked, tried and convicted.

He stripped down, neatly folded his clothes and placing them in the rucksack. Then he put the rucksack behind a fence, camouflaged by the dark.

And he changed into his Wolfman form and started to run. Over seven feet tall with claws as long as a grown man's forearm, teeth that would have shamed a saber-toothed tiger, and muscles on top of muscles. A nightmare made real, courtesy of Project Bloodborn and the United States Military.

He moved so fast that the people in the crowd saw a mere gray blur accelerating down the center of the high street towards them. Wraithlike and unreal. Insubstantial looking.

Until it struck the first deputy. A spray of blood covered all within twenty feet as the deputy seemed to be blown apart. Arms, legs and torso tearing into separate pieces from the savagery of the hit.

Then the being stopped momentarily. A mere half a second. But it was enough for those who were looking directly at it to register what was there. Two women fainted and many of the men started to scream involuntarily.

The second deputy drew his pistol with a shaking finger. Brenner blurred into movement once again, smashing the weapon from the man's grip and carrying him a hundred yards down the street, tearing him in half as he did so.

And then he was gone. Melting into the dark.

To the townsfolk it was as of the night had come alive, destroyed the deputies, laid waste to the town and then simply ceased to exist.

Brenner went right and then right again, returning to his rucksack. He picked it up and ran out of town, east into the surrounding forests. It was time to burn the remaining meth labs.

Time to spread the chaos even more.

CHAPTER 23

The two deputies lounged against the side of the fire truck. One of the firemen stood next to them. All three men were smoking. Silent, bored.

The second fireman was inside the trailer home, checking that the cook was adhering to the regulations, keeping his chemicals in separate areas, screwing the caps back on, ensuring that flammables were at the opposite end of the structure to the stove. And, on the whole, the cook was doing a good job.

The team still weren't sure why so many of the homes were exploding. It seemed obvious that a group of people must be taking them out but they had seen no sign of anyone. No strange vehicles. No tracks. Nothing.

They had questioned one of the survivors from the first explosion but the man had obviously suffered from a massive concussion. He was of Mexican descent and whenever they asked a question, he kept simply breaking down, weeping copiously and murmuring the same words under his breath like a liturgy.

'El Diablo ha venido, el Diablo ha venido.' The Devil has come.

They had left him alone, in the dark outside his burning trailer. Fucking useless wetback.

As they drove off, none of them had bothered to look in the rearview mirror. If they had, they would have seen him take out his pocket knife, open the blade and draw it firmly across his wrist.

El Diablo ha venido.

The second fireman walked out of the trailer. 'Looks fine,' he said. 'Where to now?'

One of the deputies was about to answer when a roar shattered the night air. Loud enough to feel through the soles of your feet. Both deputies immediately drew their weapons.

'What the fuck?' Shouted one.

'Mountain lion?' Questioned the one fireman.

There was a blur of movement and something crashed into one of the deputies and carried him off into the darkness. The second deputy pulled off a few shots.

They waited.

'You shot your friend, dipshit,' said a voice from out of the darkness.

But this was no human voice. It was thunder and lightning wrapped up in a version of speech. As if death itself had become carnate and decided to speak.

'What are you?' Shouted the deputy.

'I am your nightmares become real,' answered the voice.

The deputy fired again. Random shots into the dark. 'What do you want?'

'You.'

There was a rush of air and the deputies head flew from his shoulders in a welter of blood.

And the thing was gone.

After a few minutes of standing absolutely still, the firemen, with shaking hands and legs, climbed back into their fire truck and drove away, heading back for the station. They didn't even bother to wipe away the blood that covered their faces with a red viscous mask.

***

Brenner watched the SUV approaching. He had already taken out the cooker in the trailer home. A single male in his mid thirties. Brenner had knocked him unconscious and tied him to a tree some fifty yards away. For a moment he was a little worried that he may have killed him, but after checking he could feel a pulse. Weak but still there. Not that he cared that much, after all the cook was another link in the chain. A chain that had to be broken. But Brenner had not classed them as the enemy. That designation was purely for the sheriff, his deputies and whoever else was above them in the chain.

As the SUV approached Brenner saw that there were four deputies inside. And he recognized one of them. Kennedy.

The Wolfman smiled. A terrifying sight to behold.

The vehicle pulled up next to the trailer and all four deputies climbed out.

Brenner sprang into motion. Two were carrying shotguns and, as such, were designated the primary targets. They died without even knowing that their time had come.

Next Brenner smashed his giant fist into the third deputy's face, breaking his skull and dropping him to the ground like he had been head shot.

Then he grabbed Kennedy's right arm and, with a twitch of his wrist, he broke it. An horrific injury that shattered the bone and pushed the ragged end through the flesh on his forearm. Then Brenner did the same to his left, thereby nullifying any chance of the deputy drawing down on him. Finally he lifted him up by his shirt, sat him on the hood of the SUV and put his face right up close.

Then he growled.

A damp stain covered the deputy's trousers as he lost bladder control.

Brenner morphed back into his human form. Less terrifying than his lupine appearance but still six foot five and almost three hundred pounds of mighty pissed off.

'Remember me, asswipe?'

Kennedy did a double take. 'I... how... what?' His teeth started to chatter together as he went into shock, his mind simply unable to process what was going on.

Brenner slapped him. 'Snap out of it, boy,' he said.

'You tried to kill me. Why?'

Kennedy shook his head. 'Didn't.'

'Bullshit.' Another flat hand hammered across Kennedy's face.

'It wasn't me.'

'Bullshit.' This time the slap was harder, breaking the deputies nose and bringing with it a splash of bright red blood.

'I didn't mean to kill you. It was a warning. To make sure that you didn't come back.'

Brenner laughed. 'That plan didn't work out too well, did it?'

Kennedy shook his head.

'So who told you to do it?'

'Goins. The sheriff.'

'Fair enough. And who is in charge of this set up? Who be the head honcho?'

'It's Goins.'

This time Brenner's slap almost tore off Kennedy's ear. 'Bullshit. Goins couldn't wipe his own ass without a map.'

The deputy screamed in pain. 'The mayor. It's the mayor. Big house on the hill. Mayor Henry Polk. Please don't kill me. I'm sorry. I'm so fucking sorry.'

Brenner slowly morphed back into his Wolfman mode. Drawing it out so that Kennedy could see every minute change. Then he opened his jaws impossibly wide, letting the moonlight glisten off his canines.

The deputy started to keen in terror, a high

pitched formless wail of absolute horror.

Brenner's mighty jaws snapped shut.

He dropped the headless body to the ground and loped off. Heading for the house on the hill.

CHAPTER 24

Mayor Polk took another swig of his whisky. Jack Daniels Sinatra Select. Two hundred dollars a bottle. It was all that he drank. Usually he fixed it just like Frank would have. Three blocks of ice, two fingers of Jack and a splash of water.

But now he was drinking straight from the bottle. The intake of alcohol had gone from a pleasurable act to one of self-medication. A balm for his shattered nerves. As he looked out of the vast picture window on the first floor sitting room, he could see the numerous fires that lit up the night sky. At least forty of his precious trailers were burning as was the fire department and the sheriff's office.

It was a heavy blow. But he could recover. He was ambitious, cash rich, and he had a lot of well armed young men under his control.

He picked up his cell and dialed the sheriff. 'Goins. Enough is enough. I want every man that you have up here at Mount Olympus. No more fucking around. I can feel it in my gut that these fuckers are after me and the five men that you sent are insufficient protection. I want everyone and I want them now. Now!'

He disconnected the call and carried on staring out of the window. The garden before him was well lit by four huge, ten thousand watt floodlights. The area was surrounded by a twelve foot high wall and there were at least six vicious attack dogs roaming the grounds. Rottweilers and Pit bulls. The five deputies in the house with him all carried pump action shotguns as well as their customary sidearms and he himself had an AR15 with a shithouse full of ammunition.

He felt relatively safe but not safe enough. He knew that Goins had at least another twenty men with him and he wanted all of them up here with him. Protect the mayor was to be the new watchword. The new mission of every deputy.

Because without Polk there was no town of Goodbye. There was only a shitty little community in the ass end of nowhere.

He took another slug of whisky.

And then he heard the flat report of a rifle shot and one of the floodlights exploded. Seconds later the next one disintegrated in a shower of sparks. And then the next and the next. The area around the house was plunged into total darkness.

Polk dropped his two hundred dollar bottle of whisky and picked up his AR15.

'Watch the windows,' he shouted at the deputies. 'Two go to the back of the house, two to the front. One of you come up here with me.'

He heard the sound of running feet as the deputies complied with his orders. One of the younger ones, a strapping lad by the name of Curtis, ran into the sitting room. He had his shotgun ready, and he went straight to the picture window and peered out.

'Get away from the window, you dumb as shit asshole,' shouted Polk. 'There's someone out there with a rifle.'

Curtis turned to the mayor and started moving. And his head exploded as the 308 round smashed through the picture window, distorting the slug as it did so, and impacted Curtis' skull at a velocity slightly exceeding two thousand seven hundred feet per second. The exit wound took the back half of his head off and his body fell to the floor, heels drumming on the carpet as he did his dance of death.

Polk dropped to the floor and rolled, grimacing in pain as the hundreds of shards of glass form the picture window slashed into him like white hot needles.

A deputy came sprinting up the stairs and into the sitting room. 'Mayor,' he shouted. 'Are you alright?'

Before Polk could shout a warning the second deputy went the way of the first. The contents of his skull decorating the door behind him.

'No more of you assholes come running up here,' shouted Polk. 'I'm coming down.' He crawled to the door and as soon as he was round the corner, stood up and ran down the stairs. Slipping on the third last stair as he got the bottom he fell forward and rolled to a stop against the wall.

He immediately yanked his cell phone out of his shirt pocket and speed dialed Goins. 'Hey, shit-for-brains,' he screamed. 'Where are you? We're under heavy fire here.'

'Close,' replied Goins. 'How many of them?'

'How the fuck should I know?' Shouted Polk. 'I've already lost two men and haven't seen hide nor hair of the attackers. How many deputies you bringing.'

'Two car loads,' said Goins. 'Seven all told. Including me.'

'Seven? I said all of them, Goins you piece of shit. All of them.'

'That is all of them, mayor,' answered Goins. 'The rest are dead. Fucking dead. Torn to pieces, dismembered. Dead, dead, dead. So shut the fuck up and wait.'

Polk disconnected the call and stayed seated on the floor, his legs splayed out in front of him like a child in a sandpit. 'Over twenty men dead,' he whispered to himself. 'And we had yet to see who is attacking us. Who could it be?' A wave of despair washed over him. It was over. He knew now without any measure of doubt. He had been counted and measured and found wanting. He idly checked the magazine on his rifle. 'Well,' he said. 'At least I can go down fighting.'

Then the front door was smashed into the entrance hall. And in the doorway stood the devil.

Polk literally shit himself.

The monster turned to look at him, its great golden eyes like two beams of light. It sniffed the air and then shook its massive head.

'Disgusting,' it growled. 'A grown man soiling himself.'

The thing walked over to the mayor, stared down at him and then spoke again, its voice a rumbling nightmare of sound. 'Wait,' it said. 'I have some things to take care of.'

It moved, faster than any living thing should be able to. A mere blur of motion. Polk heard a gunshot and then the meaty sound of a body being torn apart. Finally, the thud of something hitting a wall at vast speed.

Then it was back, standing above him. 'I believe that I have you to thank for all the shit that goes on around here?'

Polk shook his head. 'I don't understand.'

'No,' said the thing. 'I suppose you don't. How disappointing,' he slashed downwards, his claws chopping off the top of the mayors head like a boiled egg.

Polk slumped to the floor as his systems shut down, Finally, with one last gurgle, he stopped breathing.

Brenner walked outside and into the dark. Waiting for the sheriff.

CHAPTER 25

Goins drove point, gunning the engine hard as he bounced along the dirt road that led to the mayor's house. Behind him followed another car with four deputies. Seven in total. Seven out of twenty-four. Plus the five at the mayors mansion.

Only thirteen men all told. But Goins was confident of a positive outcome. If they were all in one place, they could defend it well. No more skulking about in the dark. The enemy would have to show themselves and when they did, well, they were gonna get a truckload of buckshot up their asses.

The mayor's front gates were open. Something had torn them off their hinges and cast them aside, Probably a large truck or armored vehicle, surmised Goins as he scanned the area for the same.

But, even though it was dark it was easy to see that the area was empty and there were no tracks leading up to the gate. He skidded to a halt outside the front door and leapt out, noticing that the door had suffered the same fate as the front gate. Torn off at the hinges, the doorjamb and surrounding masonry reduced to rubble.

He turned to call his men in, and as he did so he saw a shape appearing out of the darkness. Huge and vaguely humanoid. It exploded into motion and struck the second car before anyone had exited. Smashing into it like a Mack truck T-boning a Prius. The vehicle simply folded up. Then the monster grabbed it under the front door and stood up, throwing it into the air.

The vehicle spun like a top and struck the ground with a splintering crash. Seconds later the ruptured gas tank exploded with a thump. But the sound wasn't loud enough to cover the screams of the men trapped inside the wreckage as they burned to death.

Goins called out to his remaining two deputies to follow him into the house. He turned and ran, only to slip on the floor as soon as he entered. Falling flat on his face, sliding forward as he did so. As he scrambled to his feet, he saw what had happened. The marble floor was covered in blood. Bucketfuls. And all about the hall lay body parts. Arms and legs. In the corner the remains of the mayor, an expression of absolute terror still etched on his dead face.

He turned to cover his two deputies, but they were already down. Both blood covered bodies twitching on the ground.

And standing in the doorway was a beast straight from the unholiest depths of hell.

It called his name.

'Goins. It's time.'

The sheriff raised his shotgun and fired but the beast moved like quicksilver and the shot went wide. Cycling as fast as he could, Goins carried on firing until the pin clicked dry. Then the beast ripped the empty weapon out of his hands and grabbed his throat with one of its massive clawed hands.

Goins started to pray. 'Our Father, who art in heaven...'

The creature backhanded him across the face, splitting his lips and breaking his nose. 'No,' it roared. 'You do not get to call on His mercy.'

And then it changed, shrinking before his very eyes until it was...

'Brenner,' gasped the sheriff. 'How the fuck?'

'Been hearing that question a lot lately,' said Brenner.

Goins struggled to break Brenner's grip on his throat but it was to no avail, even as a human Brenner had a grip like a steel trap.

'I don't suppose that this is going to end well?' Asked Goins.

Brenner shook his head. 'You tried to kill me. You dealt in drugs on an industrial scale. And you let your deputy violate his trust and position with a helpless lady.'

'Betty?' Asked Goins.

Brenner nodded.

'I regret that,' admitted the sheriff.

'Good,' said Brenner as he spun Goins around, wrapped his forearm about his neck and twisted.

The crack of the breaking vertebra sounded like a branch being snapped. Goins shuddered and then went limp.

Brenner dropped him to the floor and walked out. As he left, he picked up his rucksack, took out the last phosphorus bomb, ripped the tag and threw it into the mansion.

Then he changed back into Wolfman form and headed for town.

There was still one deputy left.

And he would be at doctor Hoffman's sanatorium. Three dwellings down from Morrison's house.

Covering the ground faster than a galloping pony, Brenner took mere minutes to reach the outskirts of Goodbye. Then he slowed down, trading speed for stealth. As he flittered through the shadows, heading for doctor Hoffman's house he noticed the first tendrils of light beginning to stroke the sky. The first hint of sunrise.

Moving like a ghost, the massive lycanthrope headed down the street. Stopping outside the sanatorium he sniffed the air and then padded around the back of the building. He took hold of the handle on the back door, his claws scraping on the wood as he grasped it. Then, as gently as he could, he turned it open. But his strength was not geared for such deft movements and he twisted the door handle off like it was made of putty. The door swung open to reveal a kitchen. Old stand-alone units, a nineteen sixties Formica topped table, matching chairs.

Brenner could smell alcohol. Cheap whisky. He moved through the kitchen, into a small corridor and peered into the sitting room. Slumped in an armchair, the TV on with the sound muted, was an old man. Red nose, large loose lips and sail-like fleshy ears. On the side table next to him stood an almost empty bottle of budget rye whisky, an empty glass and a dead pipe. He was snoring softly but persistently.

Brenner followed his nose; bending and turning sideways to fit through doorways he eventually found the connected wards and reception area. The reception was empty. Leading off the small area were two doors. He pushed the one open to reveal an empty room. Single hospital bed, a stainless steel table and a single cheap chair.

He turned and opened the other door.

A similar room but for the fact that the bed was occupied.

By deputy sheriff Dick Smelly.

He took one look at the Wolfman and screamed like a stuck pig.

Brenner hulked over the bed and then changed.

'Brenner. What are you?'

'I am vengeance.'

'Why? What for?'

'Betty.'

'You already crippled me. Whatever I did I have paid for.'

Brenner shook his head. 'You forced yourself on

her.'

'Fuck you,' screamed Smelly, his fear making him bold. 'I never did nothing she didn't want. She wanted me. I'm a fucking deputy.'

'No you aren't,' growled Brenner as he changed back. 'You're a fucking dead man.'

His claws slashed down, striking Smelly in the abdomen and eviscerating him with one swipe.

CHAPTER 26

Brenner walked down the center of the high street as the sun rose behind him.

The sheriff's building and the fire department were still burning, the flames low but hot. As both buildings had stood in the center of large open lots, none of the other buildings had been affected by the fire, apart from some smoke damage.

Townsfolk wandered the streets like survivors from a bombing raid. The remains of the two deputies lay scattered on the side of the high street and splatters of blood stained the surrounding ground.

Brenner turned into the diner, noting that the light was on and one of the tables had people seated at it. He walked in and was about to go to his habitual seat when he noticed who the other occupants were. Sitting in the corner. A bottle of clear spirits in front of them despite in being only minutes past sun up.

'Mister Brenner,' greeted one of the old men.

'Mister Reeve, mister Bolin,' returned Brenner as he approached the table. 'May I sit?'

'Of course, my boy,' said mister Bolin as he filled a shot glass and pushed it across.

Brenner downed it and bit back a grimace. 'What you old dudes doing here?'

They both laughed. 'We watching, boy.'

'Why?'

'That's what we do, son. We watch.'

Brenner stared hard for a moment and then shook his head. 'That ain't no real sort of answer, you do know that?'

Mister Bolin winked. 'It's the only answer you'll ever get, son. It's the only answer that we've ever given.'

'It's the only answer that you'll ever need,' added mister Reeve.

'Hey, mister Brenner,' yelled Boisy from the griddle. 'You want some food.'

Brenner shook his head. 'No thanks, Boisy. Not today. Where's Betty?'

'She out back, mister Brenner. She'll be a minute.'

Mister Reeve winked at Boisy. 'Can you fix me a Raclette?'

Boisy frowned. 'I'm sorry, mister Reeve. I don't rightly know what that is. Boisy, he be sorry, sir.'

Mister Reeve's normal half grin slipped from his face and he closed his eyes in concentration. Brenner felt a surge of power and Boisy sucked in a sharp breath.

'You know what it is now, Boisy?' Asked mister Reeve.

Boisy nodded. 'I can do that, mister Reeve but I'll

have to use American cheese. Boisy don't have no Swiss cheese.'

'Do your best, son.'

'Boisy always do his best, mister Reeve,' answered the young griddle chef.

Betty came out of the back, headed for the table and stood there, arms on her hips.

'Betty,' greeted Brenner.

She stared at him for a few seconds. 'So your mission of vengeance is over?' She asked.

Brenner nodded.

'And now what?' Asked Betty. 'You destroyed the town in the process.'

Brenner shrugged. 'Rebuild.'

'How?' Asked Betty. 'No fire station, no sheriff's office. No chicken farm. Over forty trailer homes gone. Where are they all gonna stay? Where are the people gonna work? What are we going to do? You've ruined us and you sit there like you think that you're some sort of hero.'

Brenner shook his head. 'I'm no hero. I am judgment. And the farm is fine. A bit of exterior damage. Vote for a new mayor, start a town committee, take over the farm yourselves. Live as free people instead of slaves. As for the meth cooks and their trailers. Fuck them, the only problem is that they may make trouble for the good citizens. So I suggest you get your committee going as soon as, and then vote yourself a new sheriff and a couple of deputies. This time I advise choosing people that aren't killers and rapists.'

Betty didn't answer, but she looked close to tears. Eventually she replied. 'I am thankful, Brenner,' she said. 'It's just that it all seems overwhelming. It's easy for people like you. But for normal folk, we need leadership. The scariest part of our lives is having to make decisions.'

Brenner smiled. 'You'll be fine, Betty,' he said. 'And if I had a vote for mayor it would be you, so be strong, say what you think and do what you say. Life will be hard but good. No more late night visits, no dick heads insulting Boisy, no living off the sale of drugs. It's over.'

Mister Bolin laughed.

'You find this amusing?' Asked Brenner.

'It's never over,' he said. 'Not for you Brenner. No yet at least.'

'What do you mean?'

Mister Bolin pointed outside. To the edge of town where a group of three cars was arriving.

'You got visitors,' said mister Bolin. 'And they haven't come for coffee and cake.'

***

Emile's convoy hit the dirt road on the last leg into the town of Goodbye. They were all on high alert.

'What the hell do you think went down here, boss?' Asked Virgil.

Emile shook his head. Pillars of smoke stained the sky all about them. Parts of the chicken farm were burning, two columns of smoke roiled into the sky above the town. And in the distance at least another forty separate fingers of smoke steamed up through the forest. As they turned the corner they saw that the huge house on the hill was also burning, collapsing under the onset of the flames as they watched.

'It's like Operation Shock and Awe,' said Emile. 'Like the marines bombed the fuck outa the place. I ain't never seen the like.'

The convoy pulled into the town, heading down the main street. Standing in the middle of the street was a man. Big. Tall. Wearing a checked blanket shirt, jeans and workman's boots. He was unarmed.

Emile told Virgil to stop. As they did so, Henri jumped out of the back seat and ran around to open the door for his master.

Emile stepped out, stretched and walked up to the man in the blanket shirt, noting the destruction around him as he did so. The burning buildings, the dismembered dead bodies, the blood on the street. Virgil stood on his right and Henri on his left. Amping up the intimidation level to a degree that made most men wary.

But this man simply stood and looked at them. Calm. Confident. No aggression but also not fear. A man in control.

'Can I help,' the man asked.

Emile smiled. 'Sure. Where's sheriff Goins?'

'He's indisposed,' answered the man.

'Well, perhaps I'll wait for him then.'

The man shook his head. 'Not possible. You see,

he's permanently indisposed.'

Emile raised an eyebrow. 'I see. What about mayor Polk?'

'Same.'

Emile started to realize what was happening. 'And the deputies?'

The man nodded.

'The meth cooks?'

Another nod.

'Who?' Asked Emile.

'Me.'

'You and who else?'

The man didn't answer, he simply looked Emile in the eye and Emile knew, as those two golden orbs peered into his soul, that this man had caused all of this destruction by himself. And he shivered as he remembered Mama Acadia's words.

'My child be careful. But I see strength. Power. Moonlight. A terrible enemy.'

'You are the moonlight man,' he said. 'Mama Acadia spoke of you.'

Brenner didn't reply, he simply kept his eyes on Emile, studying him.

'Darkness. Death himself walking the earth. Evil,' whispered Emile under his breath.

Brenner did a double take. 'What did you just say?'

Emile shook his head. 'It's nothing. Just something that Mama said. Something that her Loa told her.'

'Tell me,' said Brenner, his voice low, cold.

'Exactly what she said.'

Emile scowled, not used to being spoken to in such an imperious manner. 'She said, there is more. Another one. Darkness. Death himself walking the earth. Evil. He seeks the first one.'

Brenner swore. 'Shit.' He took a deep slow breath to calm himself. 'Right, this is what is going to happen. You and your men are going to leave. Now. You will never come back here. Ever. Forget about this town, forget about its people. Go now.'

Both Virgil and Henri started to walk forward but Emile held his hand up. 'There is no reason for us to stay,' he said. 'We shall leave. Not because you told us to but because I have decided to go.' He turned to face his men. 'Saddle up. We go, this place in no longer of interest to us.'

They all started to climb back into their vehicles. Emile paused just before he did. 'A question,' he said to Brenner. The big man nodded. 'What frightened you? You do not look like a man that scares easily.'

'Death himself walking the earth,' replied Brenner.

Emile nodded his understanding. 'Mama told me to be afraid.'

'Mama was right,' affirmed Brenner.

Emile waved, climbed into the car and the convoy took off at speed.

Brenner turned and went back to the diner, entering and heading back to the table in the corner. Mister Reeve was eating a plate of boiled potatoes covered in some sort of fried cheese.

'They've gone,' said Brenner. 'Now it's over.'

Mister Bolin laughed again and shook his head as Brenner sat down.

Betty appeared at his right shoulder and poured him a cup of coffee. Then she sat down.

'Those men that just left,' she said.

'No need to worry about them,' said Brenner. 'They won't bother any of you again.'

'It's too late to say that,' informed Betty.

'What are you talking about?' Asked Brenner.

'Doc Morrison.'

'What about him?'

'The room that you stayed in. The basement. That used to be his foster daughter's room.'

Brenner cast his mind back the couple of days that seemed to be months ago, so much had happened. He remembered the vaguely feminine feeling that the room gave him. 'So where is she now?'

'Those men that just left. The leader is a man called Emile Beauchamp. Mayor Polk gave Genevieve to Emile. A gift.'

Brenner frowned. 'I don't understand.'

'The Doc's wife is dying, he asked Polk for a loan for medicine and the mayor agreed. When it came time to pay it back, the Doc didn't have the money. So Polk said that he would think of a way for the Doc to sort out his debt. Then the next time that Beauchamp came visiting, he saw Genevieve in the street and commented about her. Said that she was a fine looking girl. So Polk said that he could have her. When Beauchamp left, he left with the girl.'

'But, I don't get it,' said Brenner. 'How old was she?'

'Fifteen. Sixteen now.'

'Why did the Doc let that happen? What the hell was wrong with him?'

Betty shook her head. 'Nothing was wrong with him, Brenner. He's just a normal person. The strong take from the weak. That's life. Polk told him, if he caused any problems he would kill Genevieve, his wife and him. Then he sweetened the pot by paying for the Doc's medical bills. I suppose that the Doc reckoned at least that way everyone still lived. He compromised, Brenner. We can't all destroy our enemies. Some of us just have to sit alone in the dark and take what life gives to us. But now, there's nothing to stop Beauchamp doing what he wants to Genevieve.'

Mister Bolin shook his head. 'There be wheels within wheels, boy,' he said. 'For every action there be an equal and opposite reaction. You vanquished your enemies and now look what you done. You probably killed an innocent girl.'

'Bullshit,' said Brenner. 'Don't come your guilt trip with me, old man. I didn't fuck that situation up. The Doc should have stood his ground. He should have fought.'

'He would have lost,' stated mister Bolin.

'You don't always fight to win,' countered Brenner. 'Sometimes you just fight because you have to. Because whatever the outcome it's still better than not fighting.'

'Even if you know that you are going to lose?' Asked Betty.

'Even then,' said Brenner. 'In fact, mostly then.'

No one spoke for a while.

Brenner slammed his open hand onto the table top, splitting the inch thick Oak with his blow. 'Fuck,' he yelled. 'Okay. Where does this Beauchamp live?'

'New Orleans,' answered Betty. 'That's all that we know.'

Brenner shook his head. 'Looks like I'm going on a trip.'

Betty leaned over and kissed Brenner on the mouth, the softness of her lips belying the strength of both her hands and her character.

'Before I go,' said Brenner. 'There is something that you need to know. There is a man. Solomon Hopewell. He is looking for me. I have reason to believe that he is not far behind. He will come to this town and he will ask after me. Under no circumstances will you lie to him. Tell him everything that he needs to know. Answer truthfully and hold nothing back. And be polite. Very polite. Your lives depend upon it.'

'When will he come?' Asked Betty.

'Soon. And at night. Always at night. If you follow my instructions he will not harm you.'

'And if we don't?' Asked Betty.

'You will die. All of you.'

Brenner turned on his heel and left the diner.

CHAPTER 27

Betty watched the Seven Series BMW cruise into the town of Goodbye, just as the sun went down.

It pulled up outside the diner and the driver got out, ran around the back and opened the door.

A man, dressed all in black, stepped out and surveyed the town, hands on his hips.

And then he threw his head back and burst out laughing. Genuine, deep, belly laughter.

Betty heard him say, to no one in particular. 'Brenner has been here, for sure. This is typical of the son of a bitches work.' He turned to corporal Howard who was standing next to him. 'Take a look around you, corporal,' he said. 'What do you see?'

The driver cast his gaze about. 'Fires, dead bodies.'

The man in black nodded. 'Almost fifty fires, two of them right here in the middle of the town. Two visible dead bodies, torn to bits, and I can guarantee you that there are many, many more of those about.' He shook his head. 'Man, you gotta love his work. If there ever was a man who insisted on using a chainsaw to open a can of beans, it's Brenner. Come on, let's ask some questions.'

He walked towards the diner. The driver followed.

Betty took a deep breath and waited.

Solomon walked in and doffed his hat. 'Evening ma'am,' he greeted as he held up the photo. 'Have you seen this man?'

Betty nodded. 'He said that you would come. He said to tell you everything.'

Solomon nodded. 'Yep, that would be him. Did he give his name?'

'Said he was called Brenner,' informed Betty.

Solomon sat down at one of the tables. The driver stood by the door. 'Coffee please,' said Solomon. 'And perhaps something to eat. Steak would be good.'

'Griddles broken,' said Boisy from the kitchen.

Solomon looked across and saw Boisy standing next to an obviously working griddle. He was frying eggs and burgers as he spoke. 'Looks to me like it's working,' said Solomon.

'Well it ain't,' said Boisy. 'Not for steak. Not for you, mister night-time man.'

'I'm sorry,' said Betty, her voice nervous. 'He has IDD.'

'Intellectual Disability Disorder,' said Solomon. 'Interesting. Well, unless he wants to combine that with a remarkably short life expectancy then he better start frying me some steak. Stat.'

'Boisy,' said Betty, her voice starting to shake.

'Steak for the gentleman. Please,'

Boisy shook his head. 'Griddle is broken. No steak for mister night-time man.'

'You want me to come over there, Boisy?' Asked Solomon.

Boisy shook his head. 'No.'

'Then you going to make me some steak?'

Again Boisy shook his head. 'No.'

Solomon stared at him for a few seconds and then he laughed. 'Fine. No steak for mister night-time man. I hope that coffee is not out of the question or is the coffee machine broken as well?'

Boisy shook his head. 'No steak.'

'Yeah,' snapped Solomon. 'We already established that.' He tapped the table in front of him. 'Coffee. Now.'

Betty placed a cup on the table and filled it from the Bunn flask. 'Sugar and cream?'

Solomon shook his head.

Betty turned to offer the driver some but Solomon held up his hand. 'He's fine. Now, when did Brenner leave?'

'This morning.'

'Shit,' cussed Solomon. 'So close. How long was he here?'

'Two nights,' answered Betty.

'And all these fires?'

Betty nodded. 'The sheriff told him to leave. There was some sort of altercation. They shot Brenner. Thought that he was dead. Then he came back and killed all of them, burned down their businesses and got rid of the mayor. Permanently.'

'All in one night?' Asked Solomon.

'Yes. Over fifty mobile homes, the sheriff's department, the fire station and the mayor's mansion. Also killed around thirty, maybe forty people.'

Solomon laughed again. 'Gotta admire the man. Talk about overreacting.'

'They did shoot him,' argued Betty.

Solomon shrugged. 'So what? He's a quick healer. I can't even remember the amount of times Brenner's been shot. Fifty, a hundred? Lots.' He took a sip of the coffee. 'Good brew,' he said. 'Now, where was he heading to?'

Betty shook her head. 'He didn't say.'

Solomon sighed. 'Ma'am, we were getting along so well. Now, didn't Brenner tell you to give me the truth, the whole truth and nothing but the truth?'

Betty nodded.

'Did he say what would happen if you didn't heed that advice?'

'He said that you would kill us all,' whispered Betty.

'I ask one more time, where was Brenner heading?'

'New Orleans,' said Betty. 'He's looking for a man called Emile Beauchamp. That's all I know. I swear.'

'I believe you,' said Solomon. He finished his coffee and stood up. 'I bid you farewell.' He looked at Boisy. 'Hey, chef.'

Boisy looked at him.

'Watch your back, son,' said Solomon. 'Next time I might not be in such a good mood.'

'No steak,' answered Boisy. 'Not for you.'

Solomon shook his head and left.

***

Brenner cruised down route 55, heading towards New Orleans. The knocking was getting worse, and he had stopped twice in a short space of time to top up his oil. He saw a fairly large town hear the side of the road and decided to look for a workshop.

As he hit the outskirts he drove through a semi-industrial area and soon came to a street lined with second hand car dealers, service stations and workshops. He saw one with a couple of old Harleys parked outside and he pulled in.

And old guy took a look at the hog, tutted and sucked at his teeth for a while and then said that he would need it for the rest of the day. Brenner could pick it up the next morning.

'Fine,' said Brenner. 'How much?'

The old man shook his head. 'It'll cost what it costs, son,' he said. 'You can't put a price on your hog running right.'

'Okay,' agreed Brenner. 'You know where there might be an acceptable place to bunk up for the night. Somewhere close.'

'The only place in walking distance is shitty,' answered the old man. 'It's down there,' he pointed.

'Shitty is fine,' said Brenner. 'Sounds like my kind

of place.' He took his rucksack out of the sidesaddle and set off for the motel.

As it happened, the description, shitty, was being kind. It was a classic independent motel on the skids. Empty pool, cash only, no book to sign.

'You want a towel?' Asked the check in. 'If you do its extra. Two dollars.'

Brenner nodded, took one, handed over the cash and went to his room.

Once there, he took out what looked to be a cell phone. It was actually a Thuraya XT satellite phone. The very best on the market. But unlike any normal satellite phone, this one had been rewired, encrypted and screened. It was also only capable of dialing one number. And Brenner didn't even know what that number was, he simply needed to punch in his ten digit pass code and the thing would dial automatically.

He did so and after a minute of tapping, squeaking and static sounds someone picked up.

'Ded my man, how's it hanging?'

'Hanging straight and free, Griff. And you?'

'Same old, Ded, buddy. Same old. I'm still ahead of the curve. They haven't caught me yet. Where are you?'

'Some shithole in the ass end of nowhere, don't rightly know the name of the place. But I'm heading to New Orleans. Listen, Griff, I need some info.'

'Fire away, buddy.'

'Dude by the name of Emile Beauchamp. Resides in New Orleans. I need to know whatever you can get about him.'

'He a target.'

'Could be.'

'Give me a few hours. Oh, by the way, you're in the Get Smart motel on Byway Drive in Laughington.'

'How did you do that?'

'Tracker on the phone, buddy. I like to know where my main man is.'

Brenner laughed.

'Look, Ded,' continued Griff. 'If you heading for New Orleans, you probably gonna take route 55.'

'Right.'

'I'll meet you outside a little place called Duckpond, it's a few miles before Winona. I'll send you the coordinates. We can sink some cold ones and I'll give you the info.'

Brenner smiled in anticipation of seeing his friend. 'I'll be there late tomorrow, Griff.'

Griff disconnected the call without saying goodbye.

Renner lay back on his bed. Griff was most probably his only friend. They had met in Vietnam, both sergeants, both army grunts, both Rangers. They had gotten real close as both friends and colleagues. And then *Dong re lao* had happened. That was the day that the shit had hit the fan. They had been on long range patrol, or lurps as they called them, for almost two weeks. Exhausted, dehydrated and hungry, Brenner had lost concentration for a fraction of a second and walked onto an ambush. He had been walking point and took the brunt of the fire. Struck six times in the chest with an AK. He hung onto life by willpower alone.

It was then that he had been 'volunteered' to Project Bloodborn. A black ops department that were looking for Special Forces personal to experiment on. The rest was history. He woke up in an underground hospital ward-laboratory, completely healed. In fact better than healed. He was stronger and faster by a whole order of magnitude. It was great… until the first full moon.

Long story short, he had escaped after that. Running from what they had turned him into. And Griff had helped him, smuggling him into the States in a transport plane, using his contacts to get Brenner a new life, helping him to assimilate.

And since then they had remained the best of friends, helping each other whenever help was needed.

But now Griff was an old man. Last month he had tuned seventy five. And with each year his paranoia gained strength. Griff was a true Conspiracy Theorist. From JFK to the Illuminati. From Marilyn Monroe to OJ Simpson, Griff had a theory on how the government was responsible. And if Brenner ever tried to argue Griff would simply point at him and say, 'Look what they did to you, man. Who would fucking believe that? So don't tell me that my theories are farfetched. If anything I'm not going deep enough. I've seen shit, man, and it doesn't add up.'

As a result, Griff lived alone, in a nineteen-seventy Winnebago, always on the move. The inside had been extensively customized and although there was sleeping space for two at the back and a couple of captain seats in the front with a small table, the rest was all computers, satellite uplinks and internet broadband. Griff was the ultimate hacker. But he used most of his skills looking for conspiracies. He also helped Brenner stay off the radar and furnished him with info as and when he needed it.

Happy that Griff was onto things, Brenner took a shower, changed and headed out to find a bite to eat. He asked the man at reception where the best place to dine was, but he simply shrugged and turned away.

'Thanks for the help,' said Brenner sarcastically. 'Should I mention your name to ensure good service?'

He walked towards the center of town and after a few minutes came across a bar. There was a large parking area outside, filled with motorbikes. Mainly Harley's but also some Japanese and even European models. A neon sign read, Beer. Eats.

Brenner went inside.

It was your classic local biker bar. Pool tables. Low lighting. Long counter against the far wall. An empty stage with chain link fencing in front of it. Brenner went to the bar and ordered.

'Beer,' he said. 'Anything domestic.'

The barman slid a Bud across the counter. 'You wanna glass?'

Brenner shook his head. 'You serve food?'

'Sign says we do,' confirmed the barman.

'Got a menu?'

'No. Got chili. You want?'

Brenner nodded. 'And another beer.'

You beer was cold, the chili was hot. Both were cheap and Brenner was content. He ordered his third Bud, and it arrived as a girl sat down on the barstool next to him.

'Haven't seen you around here before,' she said.

Brenner turned to look at her. Small, maybe five two. Chunky, but in a good way. Almost wholesome. Young, maybe twenty two, maybe younger. Her eyes were older. 'I'm just passing through,' he said.

'I'm Cherry, wanna buy me a drink?'

Brenner motioned to the barman and pointed at the girl. Seconds later he placed a bottle of Smirnoff Ice in front of her. Brenner slid over two twenties to cover the bill so far. The barman didn't offer any change.

'What's your name?' Asked Cherry.

'Brenner.'

'Wow, you real talkative, aren't you?'

Brenner smiled. 'Truth be, I don't have much to say.'

'That's okay,' said Cherry. 'I can do the talking. That's fine. You staying close?'

'Close enough.'

Another man walked over and stood next to the girl. He was large. Not tall, simply big. Wide, solid.

Square. 'Hey, Charlene,' he said. 'What the fuck you doing talking to this loser?'

Cherry flicked her hair. 'I told you, Bernie, I don't go by Charlene anymore. Call me, Cherry.'

'I ain't gonna call you Cherry, bitch, Cause that ain't your name. Your name is Charlene. You can't just go around making up new names for yourself whenever you want. Be reasonable.'

'Cherry,' repeated the girl. 'Not Charlene.'

The square man grabbed Cherry by the wrist and pulled her off her chair. She gasped in pain and kicked him in the shin. 'Hands off, asswipe,' she yelled.

Bernie cocked his right arm and let fly. And his fist slapped into Brenner's hand.

Brenner shook his head. 'Look, Bernie,' he said, as he released his fist. 'I just want a nice quiet drink. That's all. Cherry and I were having a chat. Nothing more, nothing less. So why don't you just fuck off for a while, I'll finish my drink and then you two can carry on with your domestic dispute after that. Fair enough?'

Bernie's face went red with rage. 'Oh boy,' he said. 'You just brought yourself a whole bucket full of whip-ass, loser. Bernie gonna teach you a lesson in manners. In fact, Bernie may just tear you a new asshole, just for fun.'

'Aw, come on, Bernie,' whined Cherry. 'Why you always gotta be such a dick? Gimme a break. Anyways, he didn't mean nothing by it. Leave him alone.'

Bernie pointed at Cherry. 'Shut it, bitch. You and I are gonna have a long talk when I finish with this loser. A long talk.'

Brenner finished his beer and then gestured to the barman. 'Another one. Thanks.'

Bernie laughed. 'Your beer drinking time is over, boy,' he said. 'Time for Bernie to give you a lesson.'

Brenner sighed. 'Go away, Bernie,' he said. 'Seriously, just leave. That way you won't get hurt. It's a win-win situation, I get to drink in peace and you get to stay out of hospital.'

Bernie sneered at Brenner and then threw a massive overhand right at him.

Afterwards people were all in general agreement that no one saw Brenner move from his bar stool. He certainly did not put down his beer. One moment Bernie was throwing a punch and the next moment he was flying through the air and smashing into the opposite wall some forty feet away.

Brenner took another sip. He didn't even bother to look at Bernie's prostrate body. Finally he spoke. 'He'll need an ambulance,' he said. 'Broken ribs, collar bone. Maybe arms.'

'No rush,' said the barman. 'It's the general consensus around here that Bernie is kinda an asshole.' He slid another Bud across the bar. 'This one's on the house.'

Brenner smiled.

CHAPTER 28

Emile opened his front door and walked inside, calling out as he did so. 'Mama. Where you be at?'

He heard footsteps coming up from the basement and Mama Acadia entered the hall. Her eyes were puffy from crying and when she looked at Emile, she froze in shock. Then, without warning, she collapsed.

Emile ran forward and caught her as she fell. Cradling her in his arms he laid her on the floor, fanning her face with his hand.

Her eyes fluttered and she looked up at him. 'You dead,' she whispered. 'I saw your death. You spoke to him and you died.'

Emile laughed. 'What I tell you, Mama? I be the baddest son bitch in the valley. Ain't no one gonna kill Emile Beauchamp.'

Mama sat up and hugged Emile. 'I don't understand, child,' she said. 'But I be happy.'

Virgil and Henri walked in. They stood close by but didn't comment on Mama's predicament.

'So tell me what happened,' said Mama.

Emile told her. About the destroyed town of

Goodbye, the death of the sheriff, his deputies and the mayor. Then finally about the man. Brenner.

Then he told her how Brenner had reacted when he had mentioned Death Walking.

Mama went pale.

'This shit ain't finished yet, Emile,' she said. 'Not by a long chalk. A storm is coming, and we had better be ready for it. Mark my words; death is coming to New Orleans.'

'We laugh at death,' said Emile.

Mama shook her head. 'No, my son,' she said. 'Death laughs at us. I say that we should take a vacation. We should spend a few weeks at the shack. Wait for this to blow over.'

The shack was the euphemistic name for a property that Emile owned in the Louisiana Bayou some two hours drive away. A five bedroom house on stilts, situated on its own island in the bayou. The only access was by boat and it was a natural fortress, surrounded by alligators, venomous snakes, bobcats and bears. Not to mention the swamp itself.

It was a place that Mama felt safe.

'I tell you what, Mama,' said Emile. 'I'll send you to the shack with some of the boys. You be safe there. But Emile gonna stay here. Ain't no one gonna be able to say that Emile Beauchamp runs from anything. Even death himself. Maybe later I come to visit. That okay?'

Mama nodded. It was the best that she could do. She just hoped that it would be enough.

CHAPTER 29

Brenner woke up as a shaft of sunlight penetrated the cheap drapes like they were mere tissue paper. He sat up and swung his legs over the side of the bed. Next to him, Cherry grunted and rolled over, pushing her face into the pillow to prevent any of the light reaching her eyes.

Brenner went to the bathroom and turned on the shower, not bothering with the hot, he merely turned the cold up full and got in. The water pressure was better than he expected and minutes later he was standing back in the room, the rented towel around his waist.

Cherry sat up, pulled the sheet to her neck and looked at him, her eyes wide. 'I didn't get a good look last night,' she said. 'Man, you are one well built SOB. You got muscles in places where most men I seen don't even have places.'

'Just a natural mesomorph I suppose,' said Brenner.

Cherry frowned. 'What you saying? You gay?'

'You really have to ask that question after last night?'

Cherry blushed. 'I suppose not. What you mean you a metamof?'

'Mesomorph,' corrected Brenner. 'It doesn't matter. You wanna shower?'

Cherry shook her head. 'No, I'll just get dressed and head on home. Should make an effort to get there before Bernie.'

Brenner raised an eyebrow. 'You live with Bernie?'

'Sure,' confirmed Cherry. 'He's okay. Got his own big rig. Earns well, hardly ever at home. He don't got no airs and graces. Things are fine.' She laughed. 'Look, he ain't no mesomorph but he'll do.'

Brenner chuckled. 'Well you won't need to rush. I reckon he'll be laid up for a couple more days at least.'

'Really?'

Brenner nodded. 'I hit him pretty hard, people usually don't recover for a few days when I do that.'

'Well in that case,' said Cherry as she let the sheet slide down, revealing a spectacular upper body. 'Why don't we take advantage of the time available?'

Brenner smiled. 'Now that is a great idea.'

***

The old guy at the Harley workshop charged Brenner one hundred and eighty dollars and as the big man gunned the engine and set off down route 55 he reckoned that it was worth every cent. The engine throbbed away like it was new born and the gears shifted as smooth as silk. Brenner twisted the throttle and set into a cruising speed a little proud of the speed limit, his eyes peeled for any signs of the highway patrol.

A couple of hours later he saw a sign to Duckpond and followed it, changing down as he hit the rougher road surface. Not long after that, the blacktop ran out, and he found himself on a dirt track.

Twenty five minutes and he saw a few buildings.

And then a sign 'Duckpond' Population 356.

He cruised into the town. At one stage it must have homed many more people than the sign suggested. But now the high street was mainly boarded up. There was a feed store. A drug store. A bar, restaurant, a barber and a service station. On the corner what looked like a mini department store. One large room filled with a plethora of various types of merchandise ranging from clothing to kitchen paraphernalia and even arms and ammunition. A catch-all retailer.

A couple of people walked down the high street and two old men sat on a sofa on the sidewalk outside the barbers. Brenner nodded at them as he rumbled past.

On the far side of the town he spotted Griff's Winnebago in a field. As Brenner got closer, he could see that his friend had patched up a cable to the power lines and had also set up an awning attached to the side of the vehicle. He sat under the awning, beer in hand. Next to him a cooler box, on the table in front a massive bag of popcorn.

Brenner stooped, kicked his stand down and walked over.

'Griff.'

'My man.'

They both started laughing, happy to see each other again.

CHAPTER 30

'So how are the Illuminati going?' Asked Brenner after his first beer.

Griff laughed. 'Fuck off, Ded,' he answered. 'We both know that the Illuminati don't exist. They're like the Knights Templar and all that shit. Bogeymen for the masses.'

'So what's new then?'

'Lots of stuff,' said Griff.

'Like?'

'You know of Pharell Williams?'

'Sure,' said Brenner. 'The dude who sang that Happy song.'

'Yep. I got proof that he's a vampire. Or some sort of immortal at any rate.'

Brenner chuckled. 'No shit?'

Griff spun his laptop around and pointed at the screen. There was a row of four photos on it. The first was a daguerreotype, blurred with sepia tones, a young man on the streets of Paris, around 1840, looking straight into the camera, a solemn expression on his face. The next was black and white, the same man in a smoky club, circa 1920 speakeasy. The third, a color photo, probably the sixties judging from the hair and clothes. The final one, a cover shot of Pharell's album. They were undeniably the same person.

'Photoshop?' Asked Brenner.

Griff scowled. 'Don't even joke, my friend. Anyway, there's more proof than the photos. I have dental records, bank accounts that have been open for over a hundred years, witness statements. He's the real deal. I'm just not sure what the deal is.'

Brenner thought for a while. 'I should go and see him. Maybe he knows how to cure me.'

'Yeah,' laughed Griff. 'Hi, mister Williams. I think that you are a three-hundred-year-old immortal. I myself am a werewolf but I don't really want to be. Can you help? Of course, stranger, why don't you go straight to the nearest madhouse and fuck off?'

Brenner shrugged. 'Well, there is that, I admit.'

Griff leaned forward, his expression serious. 'Listen, Ded. This obsession with what you call a cure. Maybe you're looking at things from the wrong direction.'

Brenner shook his head. 'Not this again, Griff.'

'Hear me out,' insisted the old man as he held up his hand. 'What do you see?'

'A hand,' said Brenner. 'Is this some sort of trick question?'

'Look closer,' insisted Griff.

Brenner did. He saw a hand. An old hand. Scarred knuckles, a couple of liver spots. The fingers swollen and warped from rheumatoid arthritis. It shook very slightly.

'You see?' Asked Griff.

Brenner nodded.

'Your curse is a gift, Ded,' continued Griff. 'I can't see so well anymore, takes me ten minutes to piss in the mornings. My reaction times have gone to shit. I'm dying. Not of any specific disease or nothing. I'm just dying like everyone else on the planet. Except for you. And Pharell Williams it seems. And I'll tell you something for nothing, my friend. Getting old sucks. It's shitty, and it's painful and it's sorta humiliating. You become invisible. Worth less than you were before. Youth is a currency and when it runs out you become one of the poor relations. So no more talk of a curse. Okay?'

Brenner nodded. 'It's the full moon that scares me. I have no control. If I can't chain myself up or lock myself away, I kill. Indiscriminately. I become pure evil.'

'Well then we need to concentrate on that. Finding a way to control the change in the first phase of the full moon. I mean, hell, Ded, its one day a month. In return you get strength, speed, and massive longevity.'

'Yeah, and a bunch of military psychos chasing me for the rest of my very long life.'

Griff chuckled. 'There is that.' He stood up, went inside the Winnebago and returned with a few A4 pieces of printed paper. He handed them to Brenner. 'Emile Beauchamp. All the relevant info. He's a player. Drugs, prostitution, pornography, illegal gambling, fight clubs. Bad dude. Fancies himself as a bit of a man about town. Has a lot of muscle and isn't shy to use it.'

Brenner scanned the notes, going back a few lines every now and then. 'Looks like he also has a few cops and politicians in his back pocket,' he said.

'As I said, he's a player,' confirmed Griff. 'So tell me, Ded, why you going for him? He insult you in some way?'

Brenner shook his head. 'It's not personal. He took a girl. Fifteen. Her father wants her back. I think.'

'You think?'

Brenner shrugged. 'I never actually asked him. But Betty from the diner asked if I could get her back. Her names, Genevieve.'

'Betty from the diner,' repeated Griff. 'You going after a drug dealing, muscled up, gun toting psycho because Betty from the diner asked you to?'

'That about sums it up,' admitted Brenner.

'Man, I hope that she was a good lay.'

Brenner shook his head. 'Wouldn't know. She did give me a kiss. She's got a brother. Boisy. He's a griddle cook. Got IDD.'

'What's that when it's at home?' Asked Griff.

'Intellectual Disability Disorder.'

'You mean, slow.'

'Sort of,' acknowledged Brenner. 'But he's different. Saw me in Wolfman form and knew who I was. Didn't scare him or nothing. He offered to cook me steak.'

'Oh, well, fine. So that's why you going on a suicide mission. Was the steak good?'

Brenner grinned. 'Boisy's a great cook.'

'Good enough to die for?'

'Everybody's gotta die sometime,' said Brenner as he opened another beer.

'True,' said Griff. 'Dull but true. Hey, I got you a present.' He headed back into the Winnebago and came out with a two foot long object wrapped in a blanket. He handed it to Brenner.

Brenner unrolled the blanket to reveal a weapon. The strangest looking weapon that he had ever seen. He held it up and inspected it. 'What the hell is it?'

'It's a shotgun,' answered Griff.

'Not like any shotgun that I've seen before.'

'It's designed for when you go Wolfman. I know that you can't use normal weapons because you go all Hulk-Smash on them and break them in half by mistake. Well this won't break. It takes a specially made 2-gage cartridge. Four barrels welded together, each with their own trigger. See, no trigger guards to get in the way of your claws. Pistol grip, manual cocking. Just don't try to fire it in human form. The recoil will tear your arm right off.'

'Is it loaded?'

Griff shook his head and handed over four brass cartridges. They looked large enough to be artillery shells. 'Adapted these from a signal cannon. Each one holds one hundred and twenty balls of double aught shot. Plus five times more powder than a twelve gage shotgun. You should be able knock a wall down with it. Or sink a boat, take out a low flying airplane. Whatever your wolfy mind decides upon. Use it wisely, that's all the ammo that I have.'

Brenner grinned. 'Thanks, Griff. I mean, some people would have thought that a sweater, or a nice pair of socks would be a great present. But this monster shotgun is a real break from tradition.'

Griff laughed. 'No one can accuse me of following the traditional routes,' he admitted as he sat down. 'look, Ded, there's one more thing. I didn't put it in the notes because, well, it just seemed a bit flaky.'

'Flaky is fine by me,' said Brenner. 'Spit it out.'

'This Beauchamp. He's got a woman. Not a lover or nothing. More like a mother. Or aunt. She goes by the name of Mama Acadia. She's a witch. Or a Voodoo priestess, or something like that.'

Brenner nodded. 'He motioned her to me. Said that she foresaw me. She also saw Solomon, said that he was looking for me.'

Griff went pale. 'Shit. If that motherfucking psycho is out there then we better move. I don't wanna be in the same state as him. Not old Griff. No sir. Damn it, Brenner. You didn't tell me that he was back on the scene.'

'Didn't know until yesterday.'

Griff shook his head. 'Anyway, this Mama Acadia. She's a priestess of note. White magik as far as I can find out, but you better be careful of her. She'll know that you coming, which sorta fucks up your element of surprise. Just thought that you should know.'

'Point taken, Griff.'

'Okay. I reckon that we can stay here tonight but I'm outta here before first light,' said Griff. 'I'm heading west. Maybe El Paso, maybe Tucson. Figure that'll take me at a ninety degree angle to wherever Solomon is coming from. Make sure that I avoid that evil SOB. And if I were you, Ded, I'd do the same.'

Brenner shook his head. 'Can't do, old friend. Made a promise.'

'Yeah,' acknowledged Griff. 'That sense of honor is gonna be the death of you.'

Brenner raised his glass. 'Mess with the best, die like the rest.'

Griff smiled. 'Rangers lead the way.'

CHAPTER 31

Mama Acadia waited for Ferdinand to open the door for her while Alphonse collected her luggage from the trunk. They were two of Emile's best boys, after Virgil and Henri, of course. Like all the muscle that Emile hired, they were big men. Fit and healthy, animalistic in their grace and strength, not academic but street smart. And like all of Emile's boys they were fanatically loyal to both him and Mama.

The humidity hit Mama like a wet sock after the air-conditioned environment of the luxury limousine but it didn't bother her. She could regulate her body temperature with ease and never sweated nor shivered with cold. Neither did any of the multitudes of bugs or mosquitoes cause a nuisance. It was easy to harden her aura to such trivialities. Even snakes and rodents wouldn't bother Mama. Alligators might prove to be a problem but that was why she had Ferdinand and Alphonse. They were there to keep the larger predators away. Both four and two legged.

Breauxtown. A one alligator pile of almost nonexistence in the middle of the bayou. Couple of shops, bait store, a bar and a few empty buildings. But it had a pier and moored to that pier was Emile's 36 foot by 16 foot Air Ranger custom airboat. One of the biggest ever made. Emile called it *Grosspork*, a bastardization of the French for Fat Pig. For some reason this amused him.

Mama hated the thing. Noisy and smelly. Not like the traditional flat-bottomed Pirogues that she preferred. But even she had to admit, the Ranger was fast and covered from the elements.

Emile had also commissioned two more 18 foot by 8 foot Enforcement models with 750 horse power super-charged engines, massive searchlights and a cabin ensconced in bullet resistant glass. It carried two men in the cabin and could accommodate another two on the deck. He had also had mountings fitted next to the passenger seat for an old WW2 Bren gun fitted with a hundred round pan magazine. Basically antiques firearms, but deadly if you were on the receiving end of them.

The small fleet was lovingly maintained and crewed by the Fournier family. An inbred collection of ne'er-do-wells that had eked out a living off the bayou before Emile had hired the entire brood as his groundskeepers, housekeepers, cooks, maids and muscle. The senior boys took care of the Air Rangers and did so with pride. They lived and died for Beauchamp and were now regarded as semi-royalty due to their proximity to the areas favorite son.

The clan numbered over thirty strong and that wasn't counting the offshoots and shirttail additions. All in all it was a well known fact that a stranger couldn't get within ten miles of Breauxtown without one of the Fournier's knowing about it.

So by the time Mama climbed out of the limousine there was already a line of supplicants on the pier waiting for her attention. People like old man Hebert who wanted Mama to make him a love potion, through to missy Benoit who wanted a curse removed. Twenty two people all told.

Mama spoke to each one and then told them that they could come across to the shack the next Morning on the *Grosspork*.

There was much bowing and clapping and even tears as Mama pulled away, waving her goodbyes. These were her people and she would treat their ills and ails the next day. She wouldn't charge them either.

But they would owe her.

CHAPTER 32

Brenner took a right off route 55 and then took the Pontchartrain Causeway across the lake. A twenty-three mile bridge with a three dollar toll charge. It was worth it. The view was spectacular and the feeling of driving over the water for so long was unique.

As he got off the causeway, he headed east on route 10, passing through Kenner and Metairie on his way to the French Quarter. He had been to New Orleans before, some twenty or thirty years back, and, although much of it was familiar, there had been some major changes so he rode around a while, simply getting his bearings and letting the feel of the city soak into him.

After an hour or so he rode past Emile Beauchamp's townhouse, slowing down and checking the place out as he did. He pulled in about a hundred yards down the street and walked back, strolling past the house and then around the block to get a closer look at the back and the houses alongside it.

While he was watching, the front door opened

and Emile walked out. He was flanked by the two walking mountains that Brenner had seen in Goodbye. They looked alert and their eyes scanned the surrounding street. Brenner faded into the shadows being cast by the setting sun. They got into a late model Lincoln Town Car that looked as if it had just rolled off the factory floor and onto the street.

Brenner jogged back to his bike and followed at a decent distance, ensuring that they didn't pick up that he was tailing them.

They didn't drive far, staying in the same neighborhood, but a couple of blocks away. Brenner wondered why they didn't walk, the weather was pleasant, the night warm with a slight breeze and no chance of rain. But then he figured that Beauchamp just wasn't a walking kind of guy. He probably took a chauffeur driven limo to cross the road.

The town car stopped outside a splendid three story residence, there was muscle at the front door and another two men walking up and down the street. Brenner stopped well clear and watched them usher Emile and his entourage inside with a serious amount of courtesy, bowing and nodding like serfs of old.

Wanting to get a closer look he walked away from the residence, scaled a wall two houses down and then made his way through the back gardens until he was next door. Then he climbed a tree, a massive Oak that must have been there before the town itself, which put it at well over three hundred years old.

He sat on a bough over half way up, well camouflaged by the dark and the abundant foliage. He had proper bird's-eye view of the garden party that was taking place in the home that Beauchamp had just entered. It looked to be some official city affair. Men in monkey suits and women in tight black dresses. Some wore gloves. There was a quartet playing Zydeco music adapted for strings.

Brenner noted a man in a police uniform, judging from his rank epaulettes, a deputy superintendent. Beauchamp was paying him a lot of attention, back slapping and laughing. Emile was obviously putting the schmooze on the cop, a point worth remembering.

And then Brenner almost fell out of the tree. Standing in the far corner of the garden were two old men. Dressed in the identical clothes that they had been the last two times he had seen them. Mister Bolin and mister Reeve. As his eyes fell on them they turned and looked directly at him, despite the fact that it was impossible to see him from where they were. Mister Reeve raised his glass in a toast and mister Bolin laughed.

'What the fuck?' Said Brenner under his breath.

Mister Bolin frowned and Brenner could read his lips as he looked at him and spoke. 'Language, boy. Language.'

Mister Reeve pointed at his own eyes and then gestured towards the crowd of revelers. It was obvious what he was saying.

We are watching.

Brenner slid down the tree and headed back to his bike before the two old men could draw attention to him. It was obvious that he couldn't take Beauchamp out in the streets. His men were too professional and the chance of collateral damage would be far too high. So it would have to be at his residence. And as that was the most likely place that Genevieve would be it suited Brenner admirably.

He parked his Harley a few hundred yards from Beauchamp's house and went in on foot. Using a similar method to the one he had just used to observe the last residence, Brenner worked his way through the neighbor's garden in order to get a closer look at Beauchamp's security measures. And there were lots of them. Brenner's enhanced eyesight picked up CCTV in the trees and on the walls. Infrared beams and even old-fashioned trip wires connected to what looked suspiciously like hand grenades but may have only been flash-bangs. He could tell by the distortion on the windows that the glass was major league stuff. At least three inches thick, which meant bullet-proof.

On the roof of the house, and above all the doors and windows were motion detectors attached to floodlights, so any movement and the garden would be lit up like midday. Added to this a bunch of guards that looked like the entire platoon of linemen from the Dallas Cowboys, meant that Brenner was looking at what might just prove to be an untenable situation.

A few hours later Beauchamp returned. Brenner caught glimpses of him as he walked around the house and he decided to wait for a few more hours. It was already midnight, but it is well known that mans lowest ebb is between three and four in the morning. This is what the hospitals call the Witching Hour as most deaths occur over this time period. Also, Brenner figured that Beauchamp would be asleep as would a few of his gourds.

Unfortunately no one told Beauchamp.

At ten minutes to four the house looked the same as it had that early evening, obviously Emile was either a night owl or simply one of those people that needed very little sleep. Brenner decided that it was time.

He took off his clothes and hung them over the branch that he was sitting on then, as soon as he had changed into his Wolfman form, he leapt across the wall and into Beauchamp's garden. With huge bounds he avoided the trip wires and the infrared beams but there was noting that he could do about the CCTV and the motion detectors. So he relied on his speed to confuse.

An alarm went off on the CCTV control room and Virgil ran in to take a look. The garden was lit up like daytime as every motion detector flicked into life, but Virgil couldn't see what had caused it. He rewound the disk and saw a blur of movement flash across the camera. He slowed it down, but it didn't help much. In fact it made it look like a massive dog, or maybe a bear, had run across the lawn and climbed onto the roof. Or maybe the first floor balcony. But the equipment must have been faulty as nothing could move that fast.

Then he heard one of the doors upstairs explode as something struck it. At the same time a fusillade of shots and one of the bodyguards screamed out at the top of his voice. '*Le Diable*. The Devil has come.'

Virgil drew his Colt 45 and ran for the steps. More shouting, screaming. More shots. The sound of an animal. Barking, howling. Grunting.

Then pleading and a death rattle.

The landing at the top of the stairs was drenched in blood. Two of Beauchamp's men lay on the floor. Virgil was about to check them for signs of like when he saw the horrific damage that had been meted out to them. Rib bones stuck out through their shirts, arms had been literally torn off and their heads were at fantastic angles that meant that they had almost been twisted off, so savage had the attack been.

'Henri,' he shouted. 'Everybody here. Look to mister Beauchamp.'

He sprinted down the corridor and kicked Emile's study door open. Beauchamp stood behind his desk, an MP5 sub-machine gun in his hand. 'What's going on, Virgil,' he demanded, his voice calm yet urgent.

Virgil shrugged and checked the window.

Henri joined them, he carried a Remington pump

action shotgun, his eyes were wild with adrenalin.

Beauchamp repeated the question.

'We're being attacked by some sort of animal,' he said.

'What?' Asked Emile. 'A bear. A fucking mountain lion?'

Henri shook his head. 'A wolf. No, a man… fuck, boss. I don't know. If it didn't sound crazy I'd say, a werewolf.'

Emile was about to repudiate what Henri has just said when Brenner appeared in the doorway. Seven foot tall, wider than the door, his muzzle dripping blood and gore, his golden eyes like searchlights into a man's soul.

Henri racked the shotgun and fired but Brenner didn't even flinch as he advanced. Three more bodyguards ran into the corridor and started firing as well, forcing the Wolfman to turn and dispatch them. He grabbed the one by the neck and smashed him into the other two. Using the man's body like a massive blunt weapon to bludgeon them to the ground.

Virgil used the distraction to shepherd Beauchamp out of the window and onto the balcony. He pulled down a fire escape ladder that led to the roof and helped his boss onto it, finally turning to his brother.

'Henri, slow that thing down. I need to get the master to safety. I'll see you at the shack.'

Henri nodded and turned to face the Wolfman. As Virgil disappeared up the ladder, pulling it up after him.

Brenner entered the room again. Behind him the house was silent. The bodyguards had all been dispatched.

'Move or die,' he growled at Henri.

The big man shook his head. His gaze was calm. No fear.

Brenner nodded and then changed back onto human form. 'I will fight you as a human,' he said.

Henri bowed slightly. 'Thank you for the privilege.'

The two men faced each other for a few seconds. Sizing one another up. Henri was bigger. Much bigger. But Brenner's naked body displayed a musculature that was superhuman. Ripcords of muscle overlaid with scars and underlaid with solid bone and tendons. Not an ounce of superfluous flesh.

They both burst into movement at the same time, throwing punches, ducking, weaving, kicking.

Henri launched a combination of punches at Brenner, a straight left, followed by a right hook and then a left uppercut. He was blisteringly fast but although every punch got close, none actually landed. Even in human form, Brenner was preternaturally quick. He didn't anticipate or guess. He didn't need to. He simply waited for Henri to throw a punch, or launch a kick and then he responded, moving out of the way and counterpunching.

He struck Henri in the ribs. Two solid blows in

rapid succession and he heard the crackle of the ribs breaking.

Henri went pale as he absorbed the punishment, falling to one knee as the air rushed out of him. Brenner stood back and waited for the big man to regain his breath. After a few seconds, Henri nodded and stood up again.

He kicked low, seeking to smash Brenner's knee, but Brenner twisted to the side and swept Henri's other foot out from underneath him, following up with an elbow to the bridge of his nose as he fell to the floor.

Once again, Brenner waited for the big man to rise to his feet. But this time, Henri swayed from side to side, his eyes unfocused, blood pouring from his nose.

He waited for almost half a minute before nodding and launching another attack. This time Brenner stepped in close and punched him in the gut, a savage uppercut, looking to tear the stomach muscle away from the wall and rupture internal organs. Henri staggered back but managed to stay upright. He held up his right hand.

'Wait,' he gasped. Then, after a few seconds he shook his head. 'Finish it,' he said. 'Do me the honor of not holding back any more.'

Brenner nodded and waited for the big man's final attack.

As Henri threw a massive overhand right, Brenner stepped inside and struck him below his left ear. The blow was hard enough to throw the big man across the room and the crack of his neck breaking sounded like a gunshot.

He was dead before he hit the floor.

Brenner changed back into Wolfman mode, ran onto the balcony and scaled the wall up to the roof. But Beauchamp was long gone as Brenner knew that he would be. But he could not have done it any differently. Henri had deserved a more even fight. He was a brave man who had shown no fear, and in Brenner's book that commanded a measure of respect. Even of it had meant that Beauchamp had to get away.

For now.

Brenner took a deep breath and headed back into the house, ready to find Genevieve.

First, he checked the top two floors, kicking open doors and looking into each room but they were all unoccupied. One of the rooms was obviously Henri's, or perhaps Virgil's, judging by the clothes laid out on the bed. Brenner picked up a pair of jeans and draped them over his shoulder to put on later. Then he continued his search by scouted out the first floor. But that was all reception rooms and a kitchen.

Finally he found the steps leading to the lower ground floor. The basement. At the foot of the stairs was a small landing, a door on the right and a corridor on the left. Brenner chose the corridor. At the end if it was a door, two locks, reinforced hinges. He balled his fist and punched it into the room, taking care not to not to strike it too hard in case it hurt someone as it flew off its mountings.

He walked in, hunching over and turning sideways to fit. His entrance was greeted by a trio of screams.

There were three girls. All young. All dressed in lightweight dresses in a diaphanous material that clung to their figures and displayed their lack of underwear in an obvious, fashion. All screaming.

Brenner dropped to one knee and lowered his head to show his lack of aggression. Then he changed back into his human form, stood up and put on the jeans. They were slightly too large, but they had an attached belt that he pulled tight.

He glanced around him. The place reeked of opulence, Persian rugs, original artwork, fresh flowers and subtle hidden lighting. The furniture was a blend of seventies classics and Edwardian club. Milo Baughmann chairs, leather Chesterfields and Sheraton display tables.

These girls may have been prisoners, but they were living in the veritable lap of luxury.

'Who, and what, the fuck are you?' Asked one of the girls.

'My name is Brenner, which one of you is Genevieve?'

The girl who had asked him the question took a tentative step forward. 'That'll be me,' she answered.

'You're free,' said Brenner.

None of the girls spoke for a few seconds.

Finally Genevieve said. 'Free to do what?'

'Whatever you want,' said Brenner. 'Free to go home. In fact I'll take you.'

'Seriously?' Asked Genevieve. 'Free to go back to Ass-ville in the middle of nowhere? Free to go back to Captain Coward, the fuck face who let them take me even though he claims to be my father? Free to go back and watch him mope himself to death as he wallows in a mire of self pity? Why would I want to do that?'

Brenner did a double take. 'I thought that you might like to see your dad. Live a normal life. Not locked up in a basement and being taken advantage of whenever someone else feels like it.'

'He's not my dad,' snapped Genevieve. 'And she's not my mom. He let the mayor give me away like I was a fucking wheelbarrow or a snow shovel. He let those deputies do whatever they wanted. Night after night. Those, dirty, unwashed hillbilly motherfuckers. At least Emile cares for me. I am still a commodity but at least I am a precious one. I have value.'

She burst into tears.

'Don't blame your foster-dad, Genevieve,' said Brenner. 'Not all men are made to fight back. Not all men resort to violence. Some simply do not know how to. They are incapable of it. He alone cannot shoulder all the responsibility. There were others in the town that also didn't fight back. Others that stood to one side and watched. Maybe it's time to forgive. Not to forget, that will never happen, but you can forgive. And in doing so you shall be set free.'

'He's not my dad. So you can fuck off, mister holier than thou. I'll wait here for Emile thank you very much.'

'Well you'll wait for a long time,' said Brenner, 'because very soon he's going to be dead. Just like everybody else in this house is dead. He has done wrong and I am going to find him and exact retribution.'

Genevieve said nothing. Neither did the other two girls.

Brenner shook his head and walked out. 'Oh, by the way,' he said as he was leaving. 'Betty says, hi.'

'Wait,' called out Genevieve. 'How is she?'

'Fine,' answered Brenner. 'Well she will be soon. The town's undergone a few minor adjustments since you were last there. The sheriffs dead, so is the mayor and all the deputies. A few of the meth cooks as well. The sheriff's department and the fire station have burned down and, as far as I know, they're looking for a new mayor and sheriff.'

'How?' Asked Genevieve.

'They made a tactical error.'

'You?'

Brenner nodded.

'They treated us like chattels,' said Genevieve. 'The deputies. Raped me many times. Different ones. The sheriff knew. Condoned it. Youthful exuberance he called it.'

'I'm sorry,' said Brenner. 'If it helps, they died hard. They suffered. Every last one of them died in screaming terror.'

A tear ran down Genevieve's cheek. She smiled. 'It does help,' she said. 'I know it shouldn't but it does. Those fucking animals.'

'You can't stay here, Genevieve,' said Brenner. 'It's over. I'm going for Beauchamp and he won't survive. Afterwards, if I can help I will.'

'I don't need help,' said Genevieve. 'We don't need help,' she took in the two other girls with a gesture. 'I have money. Loads. Well, not mine but if Emile isn't coming back, I suppose that it is now.'

'Whatever you want you can take,' said Brenner.

'So, you going after Emile? Do you even know where he is?'

Brenner shook his head

'There's a place he calls the shack. I think that it's in the Louisiana Bayou somewhere, that's all I know. He'll be there. So will Mama. And she'll see you coming, Brenner. She sees all. Be careful. I'll find my own way home.'

Brenner nodded. 'Good. Hey, one last thing, there's a deputy superintendent. Don't know his name, seems to be pals with Beauchamp. Know anything about him?'

Genevieve nodded, 'That would be mister Surpas. Soppy Surpas. Yeah, Beauchamp brings him around here often. Lets him use us.'

'Why soppy?'

Genevieve laughed. 'He cries after he fucks us, gets all religious and talks about his wife and how he's doing a terrible thing. Then he's back a couple days later, doing it all again. What an asshole.'

'Where's he live?'

'Dunno, look it up on the internet, phone book, whatever, I ain't a detective.'

'Sure, no worries.'

Genevieve walked over and gave Brenner a kiss on the mouth. 'Thanks,' she put her hand on his chest. It was warm. Tiny. Like a child's.

Brenner nodded and left without looking back.

CHAPTER 33

Brenner got lost looking for the suburb of Harahan and ended up on the wrong side of the river, so he had to take the Huey P Long Bridge back into Elmwood. He rode past the Walmart and took a left, finally getting his bearings.

It hadn't taken him long to track down Deputy Superintendent Mike Surpas' address. The internet was a great tool. He figured that Surpas was buddy-buddy enough with Beauchamp to know exactly where his shack was and so it was time to pay the man a visit.

He stopped his bike opposite the given house and kicked the stand down. It was a big double story in the most expensive part of Harahan, a mere twenty minutes from the center of New Orleans. A large plot nestled alongside the Mississippi River, in-out driveway, two late model cars and well-manicured gardens. All in all, about fifty percent more house than a deputy superintendent should be able to afford.

Brenner got off the Harley and headed for the house.

Inside, Mike Surpas was looking forward to an evening alone. His daughter had gone back to Louisiana State in Baton Rouge and his wife was visiting her sister who had just moved to Lake Charles with her new husband, the fourth in the series, as it were. He strolled into the kitchen and grabbed himself two bottles of NOLA Blonde, his favorite local beer. Then he went through to his den and was about to sit down when someone spoke to him.

'One of those beers for me?'

Surpas started and dropped the second bottle. There was a blur of movement and someone caught it, pushed him back into a chair and then stood over him. A big man. Golden eyes that looked right through you.

Deputy superintendent Surpas was no coward, but he was also a pragmatic man. And that's why he could afford a house that cost only a little shy of one million dollars. And he knew that this man in front of him was not to be taken lightly. It was obvious that this was a man that needed to be treated with respect. And a healthy dose of it at that. He positively reeked of tightly controlled aggression and power.

'What do you want?' Asked Surpas.

'Information.'

'You can get whatever you need at the station.'

'Information on Emile Beauchamp.'

Surpass shook his head. 'Who?'

Brenner said nothing, he simply walked around

the den, looking at the trophies, pictures, cd rack. Then he picked up a baseball bat. 'Nice bat. Thirty two ounce?'

Surpass nodded.

'Not cheap,' continued Brenner. 'Maple. Handmade.' Without any sign of effort he snapped the bat in half, then he grasped the separate halves and snapped them again, throwing the four pieces on the floor.

'Oops,' said Brenner. 'Now, where were we? Oh yes. Beauchamp. We had a bit of a run in earlier on. He got away. Rumor has it that he's hiding out in a place he calls the shack. Louisiana. I need to know where, exactly it is.'

Surpas looks at the shattered pieces of hardwood and nodded and told Brenner where the shack was as well as the best ways to get there.

'Good,' said Brenner. 'Well done.' He looked around a little more. 'Tell me, Surpas. What's this place worth?'

'Not sure,' answered Surpas. 'About a mill.'

'What's the mortgage every month?'

'With taxes, around five thousand dollars a month.'

'I assume that Beauchamp pays it.'

Surpass saw no reason to lie. After all, the man with the golden eyes obviously knew the answer. 'Yes,' he admitted. 'Beauchamp pays the mortgage. He also pays for my daughter's college. In return I keep trouble away from him. He stays clean and I take care of my family. No harm done.'

Brenner shook his head. 'No harm done? I should kill you just for saying that, you whore mongering, drug dealing piece of shit. But I've killed more than my share tonight so I'm gonna let you live. Some advice though, I'd look at selling up. Real soon. Beauchamp is gonna be outa business and you gonna find yourself with a serious cash flow problem. Just a sound piece of financial advice. Oh, and if I happen to come back this way again and I find you with your hand in the cookie jar.' Brenner leaned in close, his face inches away from Surpas. And he allowed a slight change. His jaw lengthened, his teeth grew and a layer of fur covered his face.

Then he growled.

Surpas squeaked like a terrified mouse.

'Clean up your act,' rumbled Brenner.

He left via the front door.

Surpas didn't move for almost a minute and then he broke down and started whimpering in fear.

CHAPTER 34

Brenner woke early, before first light. He had stopped in a small place some forty miles from Breauxtown, the town that serviced Emile Beauchamp's island retreat. Unlike his usual down-market choice he had booked into a small bed-and-breakfast. The owners, an old couple who spoke English with such broad Cajun vernacular that he had to concentrate like he was taking his SATS again just to get the gist of the conversation.

Upshot of the matter was that he ended up in a comfortable, clean room with an adjoining bathroom and clean bedding. More than he could have hoped for.

After his morning shower, he went to the dining room for breakfast. The lady of the house set a massive plate of Cajun Breakfast Casserole down in front of him with a jug of coffee. The food was spectacular. Thinly sliced Andouille sausage, peppers, eggs, cheese, onions mixed together into a mélange of perfection. As soon as Brenner had finished his plate, she piled it high again and then a third time, after which she rest her hand on his shoulder, nodded and grinned in approval.

Finally she brought him a wedge of Apple-Pecan baked oatmeal. Brenner polished his plate off and then sat back, a huge grin on his face.

After a pause to allow his digestion to catch up he packed, paid up and left, confirming that he was still heading the correct way to get to Breauxtown just before he went. When he glanced in his rear view mirror the old lady was still waving at him until he turned the corner.

Taking the back roads, he passed through a score of villages that were little more than a bait shop and two houses, or a bar and a church, with names like Anacucu and Ticfoha and Shongalooah. The last one boasted a sign that read, 'If you lived here then you'd be home now'.

After another ten minutes of riding he had to admit to himself that he was lost. The roads were no better than dirt tracks and the last two towns that he had come across didn't even have name signs.

Up ahead he saw another settlement. Four houses, an all purpose shop. He stopped outside the shop, kicked down the stand to the Harley and walked in.

All of the merchandise was stacked on floor to ceiling shelves behind the service counter. Apart from a wheezing old coke fridge and an equally decrepit ice chest that took pride of place in the center of the shop floor,

The man behind the counter was counting out

fishhooks and putting them into plastic pill containers. He finished his task and looked up. 'What can I do you for, *mon amis*?'

'I'm lost,' admitted Brenner. 'Looking for Breauxtown. Can you tell me where it's at?'

Brenner could see the man's eyes glaze over as he registered the question and then hesitated slightly before he answered. 'Never heard of no Breauxtown, *whodi*. Sure you got the name right? There be a place near enough called Brotaine. It be some fifty miles due east from here.'

Brenner stared for a while, allowing the tension to build. Unblinking, his eyes crackling with restrained power.

The man started to sweat. Fat drops sliding oil-like from his hairline and down his face.

'You wouldn't lie to me, my friend?' Asked Brenner.

The man shook his head. Rapidly from side to side like a child trying its best to convince a parent that they had nothing to do with the crayon drawing on the lounge wall.

'What's your name?' Asked Brenner.

'Clovis Foret.'

'How old you, Clovis Foret?'

'Some fifty seven year old, *monsieur*.'

'You wanna live to be fifty eight?' Asked Brenner, his voice low and soft. Earnest.

'I would greatly appreciate that, *monsieur*.'

'You obviously know who I am,' said Brenner. 'What did they tell you?'

The man went pale and his eyes started to dart around the room.

'Don't be afraid,' said Brenner. 'Not yet. I'll tell you when to be afraid, until then you be okay. Just tell the truth. What did they say about me?'

'They told that you were a *Rougarou, and* that you was coming to kill the master.'

'*Rougarou*,' repeated Brenner. 'I've heard this word before. Shapeshifter?'

The man shook his head. 'Werewolf.'

Brenner shook his head. 'I wish that they'd get their facts straight,' he growled. 'I'm a fucking military experiment, not a werewolf. Anyway, I assume that the master is Emile Beauchamp?'

'Yes, *monsieur*.'

'Do you believe them, Clovis?'

Clovis nodded. 'Of course. It be said that Mama Acadia can turn into a bird. So why not someone who can turn into a wolf? Truth be, *monsieur*, that shit goes down all the time in the bayou. Or so it's said.'

'Not so sure of that, Clovis,' denied Brenner. 'Whatever, tell me how to get to Breauxtown or things are going to go mighty hard for you. And in case you were wondering, now is the time to get scared.'

As the man opened his mouth to answer, Brenner heard the unmistakable sound of a pump action shotgun being racked. As the weapon fired, he threw himself sideways and rolled, ensuring that the attacker missed.

Unfortunately, Clovis was not so fortunate, and his head was torn apart as the charge of double aught ripped through him.

'Oh shit!' Brenner heard someone shout from the doorway. 'I just shot, Clovis inna face.'

'Why?' Yelled someone else.

'The *feet pue tan* jumped out the way. Never seen anyone move so fast in my entire goddam life. He's like shit outa a goose.'

'Where is he now?'

'I don't know.'

'Well come back into the street. The boys are coming with some serious firepower, we'll take this *cowan* out.'

Brenner heard the sounds of running feet as more people approached. 'Shit,' he murmured to himself. 'Looks like the welcome committee just got bigger.' He cursed himself inwardly for underestimating the influence that Beauchamp held in the area.

The info that Griff had dug up mentioned that Beauchamp was well liked in the Bayou but not that he was almost worshiped. This was bad. And it looked like Brenner was going to have to fight his way to Breauxtown before the real battle even began.

After a quick internal debate, Brenner decided to go full Wolfman. After all, the people from this piece of shit town seemed to already know about him and there was no way to get out of the situation with some help from the beast. Without taking his clothes off, he simply changed, shredding the jeans and shirt as he did so. Then he clambered swiftly up the shelves until he was at the top. Extending his claws he tore a hole through the ceiling and climbed out onto the roof, keeping low so that no one would see him from the street.

He slithered across the wooden shakes and peered out into the street below. There was already a crowd of around ten men, all armed. One was carrying what looked like an M16, the rest had bolt action rifles or shotguns.

Brenner hated fighting assault rifles, so the man with the M16 had just upgraded himself to public enemy number one. He had to go first. Without any warning Brenner leaped from the roof and came crashing down on the man with the assault rifle. A quick twist and the man fell to the ground, his head facing the wrong way. Then Brenner grabbed the rifle by the barrel and lay into the crowd, using it as a blunt weapon.

Everybody opened up at the same time. But it was impossible to hit the thing that was blurring from place to place like a magic trick. Bones broke, arteries were severed and the residents of the no-name town participated in an unhealthy amount of friendly fire, just to add to the absolute chaos.

Ten seconds later Brenner stood alone.

He threw his head back and howled in frustration. 'I only wanted fucking directions,' he yelled out to no one in particular. 'What the hell is wrong with you people?'

A shot rang out and Brenner felt the shock of a round striking his shoulder. But instead of going down he spun and leapt at the gunman, snatching the rifle from their hands and casually breaking it in two before letting out an almighty roar that shook the surrounding buildings.

It was a woman. Probably mid twenties, maybe a little younger. Blue-black waist length hair and sapphire eyes. She was wearing a dress that was a little too tight and had been washed thin over time. Her teeth chatted in terror as she looked up at the seven foot Wolfman looming over her. But she did not drop her eyes or cower.

Then she spat at Brenner.

The Wolfman rolled his eyes. 'Really,' he grunted. 'Spitting. What is it with you dudes? I mean, where is all the anger coming from? I just want to get to Breauxtown. That's all.'

'Rougarou, satan,' said the girl. 'You come to take away our master. Our livelihood. Why?'

Brenner had finally had enough. Everything he did, people were carrying on like he was the bad guy. It was end of the tether time. Reaching out carefully he grabbed her by the throat. 'Now listen girl,' he said, slowly and succinctly, his massive jaws chewing on each syllable. 'Tell me where Breauxtown is or I will burn this shithole town to the ground. Then I will kill every person that lives within a ten mile radius. Do you understand?'

The girl shook her head. 'You won't.'

'I fucking will. I swear it.'

She looked at him for a few seconds and then nodded. 'I believe you,' she said. 'You are filth.'

'Yeah,' agreed Brenner. 'Whatever. Breauxtown?'

She pointed down the road, west. 'Ten miles then the road forks. Go left then left again. There is no other town on that road. Are you going to kill me now?'

Brenner dropped her. 'No,' he growled as he walked off. 'But if you shoot at me again, I will rip your arms off and you can take your chances from there.'

Brenner changed as he walked. Then he stopped by his Harley, pulled some clothes from his saddle bag, put them on and left.

The girl watched him go, and then she pulled out a cell phone and dialed. 'He was here,' she said. 'He killed all of them. With ease. I shot him with my rifle but he didn't even seem to notice. He's coming. I sent him the long way round so tell them to get ready.'

She disconnected the call and then sat down and started to shake uncontrollably as reaction caught up with her.

CHAPTER 35

Beauchamp cast his gaze over the men and women standing in front of him. Thirty-four of them including the men that he had brought from New Orleans. Thirty men and four women, all hard, tough and rough. All loyal.

In addition to these people, the patriarch of the Fournier family, Bruno, had promised another ten hardy souls to join them in Breauxtown in order to stop Brenner getting to the island. Beauchamp had supplied weapons for them as well.

Emile had opened his substantial armory and issued every person with a either an M1 Carbine or a Thompson sub-machine gun. Beauchamp had purchased the weapons some ten years before, from a dealer that was looking to unload a large amount of Second World War ordnance at a bargain basement price. It was at the same time that he had gotten hold of the two Bren guns that were mounted on the two Air Rangers. It was old weaponry but still deadly. Lethal enough, in fact to have still been used in the Korean War and well into Vietnam.

'A man comes today,' said Beauchamp as he stood in front of his people. 'But this is no ordinary man. This is a *Rougarou*. A demon. The spawn of Satan. And he comes to strike us down. He comes to take what is rightfully ours. He comes to destroy our families, our way of life and our children's future.' He paused for effect. 'But we will not allow him to do that.'

The people cheered and raised their weapons in the air.

Beauchamp pointed to Bruno Fournier. 'Papa Bruno. I need eight of your men on punts. Four boats, two men each. Close patrol around the island. Then six men on the two Air Rangers. Driver, Bren gun and rifleman on each. Leave another ten men on the island with me and my boys. Then you take whoever is left to the town. I want you in charge. If this *Rougarou* motherfucker gets to Breauxtown, you kill him. If he slips past you, then the boats will get him. If not, well he signs his own death warrant the moment he steps a foot on the island.'

Again everyone cheered.

'Go to it, *mon amis*,' shouted Beauchamp.

Virgil walked over and stood by his master's side. The big man was quiet. His expression blank but his eyes filled with a burning hatred. The *Rougarou* had killed his twin brother and nothing mattered until the devil spawn was dead. 'Boss,' he said. 'I have set up two ambushes on the road here. I'll be surprised if that *kawin* even gets to the town.'

'Mama Acadia says that he will come. Whatever traps we set, we shall have to face him.'

Virgil shrugged. 'Good. Let him come.'

Emile patted his bodyguard on the shoulder. 'I agree, let him come and we will kill him. Now go and ensure that the island is well covered.' Beauchamp watched his man walk off and then he went back up to the house, entering via the back door and heading for the kitchen to get a cold beer.

Mama was waiting for him in the kitchen. Emile hadn't seen her since the early morning as she had been communing with her loa and preparing spells of protection for him and Virgil.

She waited for Emile to slake his thirst before she spoke. 'You have done all that you can,' she said. 'But I have one more task for you.'

'What would that be, Mama?'

'The men in the punts. I need them to chum the waters close to the island. Fish guts, meat, whatever, I want the water thick with it. Starting at sundown. He will come tonight, under the cover of the dark.'

'Mama, if we chum the waters it will attract every alligator in Louisiana. The waters will be alive with them.'

Mama Acadia nodded. 'Yes,' she agreed. 'And they be my friends, them *cocodrie* will do my bidding, and then, Wolfman or not, he be no match for a hundred *cocodrie*.'

Beauchamp smiled and toasted Mama with his beer.

***

Corporal Howard stopped the BMW outside the bed-and-breakfast and turned off the engine. 'This is the place that the man at the gas station directed Brenner to,' he said. 'It's the only place in the town that offers rooms.'

Solomon chuckled. 'The day that Brenner trades that old rat bike of his in for some generic piece of Jap Crap is the day our lives would get more difficult. It must be one of the more recognizable forms of transport around.'

Howard nodded his agreement but remained silent.

'Right, corporal,' said Solomon. 'Sun's a bit high in the sky for me. This one's on you. No need to fuck around, we know he was here, just find out when he left and where he was going. Any shit, you break a few bones. You think that you can handle that?'

'Yes, sir,' answered Howard. 'I have done this before.'

'Watch the attitude, corporal. Now move.'

The driver got out of the BMW, walked up the front stairs and went inside. The entrance hall had a desk with a chair behind it. No one was there but there was small silver bell on the desk. He rang it and heard approaching footsteps almost straight away.

An old couple entered via the corridor, both were smiling.

'Can I help, mister?' Asked the man.

Howard held up the photo. 'When did he leave and where was he going?'

The old man was about to answer when the lady shook her head. 'Never seen him,' she said. 'Sorry, we can't help.'

'Don't do this,' said Howard. 'We know that he was here. Now, answer truthfully and nothing will happen to you. But if you continue to lie, then I shall be forced to call my colleague. That would be a fatal incident.'

'You would kill and old lady for not answering a question?' She asked.

Howard shook his head. 'No. But he would. In fact he might do so anyway, if I take too long. So I am begging you, please.' He held up the photo again.

The old lady sighed. 'He left early this morning. He asked directions to Breauxtown. I told him that he needs to keep heading west. That's all.'

The driver bowed. 'Thank you, ma'am.' He left and got back into the car. 'Heading for a place called Breauxtown,' he said. 'Left early this morning.'

Solomon rubbed his hands together. 'Happy days.'

CHAPTER 36

Brenner had walked point, countless times in Vietnam. And he had lived. It was a well-known belief that you either lasted one day on point or you made it through your tour. And that was because the grunts with that extra something, that unquantifiable ability to react faster than the average soldier, survived. Those who didn't… died.

Because combat is measured in microseconds. It takes mere fractions of a second to pull a trigger. A bullet travels at over three thousand feet per second, traveling its kill distance in an ambush in literally a millionth of a second.

So the difference between living and dying can be counted in the very tiniest of increments. The living man is merely the one who reacted one millionth of a second before the man that died.

A harsh reality of mortal combat.

Brenner dropped the Harley into a slide as the fusillade of shots buzzed and cracked through the air where he had been mere microseconds before.

Ambush.

He rolled hard and fast, changing even as he did

so. By the time he was in the brush on the side of the dirt road he was in full Wolfman mode.

And the carefully laid ambush became a killing field for the beast.

There were five men. Three on the right side of the road and two on the opposite. Brenner ended up amongst the three. Moving at whirlwind speed he tore into them, slashing and biting. Two went down instantly but the third drew a large Bowie knife and stood in a fighting stance, still but ready to move.

Brenner was impressed. Although tall, the man was not large. Long, ropey muscles as opposed to massive slabs of power. A man built for speed and reach. The perfect knife fighter's build. They stood watching each other for a few seconds because, unlike the movies where knife fights are well choreographed ballets of movement involving clashing blades and men ducking and weaving, real knife fights are short, sharp and deadly. Seldom do they last more than two or three strikes. Often only one.

Brenner could have simply used his superior speed and strength to overwhelm the man but his innate sense of respect caused him to at least allow him a fighting chance. Both watched the others chest and hands, because that is where a movement originates. Not the eyes, but the chest or hands. The man flicked the blade from his left to his right hand and stepped forward, sweeping it upwards in a low underhand strike, aimed for

Brenner's gut.

Instead of moving away or jumping to the side, Brenner stepped forward and blocked the man's arm by striking his elbow with an open hand. The knife dropped from nerveless fingers as his elbow shattered. Then the Wolfman ripped his talons up and through the man's neck. Two movements. Strike, counter-strike.

More bullets screamed and spat overhead as the two men on the other side of the road opened up, no longer nervous of collateral damage. The sound of the M1's caused Brenner a momentary flashback to Vietnam as he gathered himself and leapt across the road, jumping over twelve feet into the air and landing directly on top of one of the gunmen, snapping his neck as he did so. The final ambusher lost his nerve and turned to run, but his retreat was to no avail as the Wolfman slashed his tendon to bring him down and then, with a savage crunching of teeth, crushed his skull.

Brenner changed back to human form, retrieved his ripped and tattered jeans, pulled them on, mounted his Harley and continued on towards Breauxtown.

CHAPTER 37

The sign read, Breauxtown–3 miles.

Brenner pulled his Harley over and wheeled it into the bushes on the side of the track. From here on in, he was on foot. First, he loaded his wolf-gun into his backpack, then a change of clothes. Finally he adjusted the straps and changed into full-wolf mode, the best mode for traveling through the swamp and bush. Sliding his head through the straps, he let the pack settle around his neck and started to run, moving through the bush like a wraith.

As he ran the shadows began to lengthen and the setting sun bathed the sky in a stained glass glow. He smelled the second ambush long before he saw it. Like the first one, it was set on both sides of the road. Two men in each team.

He sped up, breaking into a full sprint and hitting the two on his side fast and furiously, massive jaws tearing and crushing. Then, without pause, he leapt across the road with one bound and dispatched the second team.

Not a shot had been fired. In fact, not one of the

men had even moved from their positions, dying where they had waited to spring their ambush.

Brenner was the beast in the night and he was hunting.

The top of the food chain had arrived.

The night had fully enveloped the land, and the swamp came alive as the chorus of tree frogs harmonized with the bass line of the bullfrogs. Barred owls played the lead while the susurration of millions of insects tied the night choir together with an ever-changing backdrop of clicks and chirps.

And above all, every now and then, the booming grunt of an alligator.

Minutes later Brenner hit the outskirts of the town and, as he did so, he changed to human form, grabbing his change of clothes from the backpack as he did so.

Then, eschewing any pretense of subtlety he simply stood tall and walked down the middle of the main street, all senses on full alert.

Breauxtown was slightly larger than some of the other no-horse towns that he had recently ridden through. And not quite as shabby.

A group of maybe twenty houses, a drug store, a service station and a bar. A pier with a workshop on it that sold bait and cold beer. A couple of pickups made up of equal quantities of paint and rust.

The Wolfman could smell people. Many people. But he could not see any.

He wandered over to the bait shop at the end of the pier; he figured that they would know where

Beauchamp lived. But, although the shop was open for business there was no one there. A small hand written sign on the counter read, *Help yourself to bait, prices marked. Put your money in the tin. This means you, Vernon!*

Brenner walked back along the rickety wooden structure and headed to the bar. Pushing open the double swing doors he went in. It was dark, smelled of stale beer and fried food. No air-conditioning. Instead, a series of ceiling fans spun lazily overhead, pushing the hot damp air around like a sheep dog herding sheep. They made no appreciable difference to the temperature. Four men sat at a central table. There was a deck of cards in the middle but it was untouched. Two more sat at the bar.

Behind the counter the barman was obeying the unwritten law of bars the world over as he polished a glass with a rag that looked like it was an experiment in germ distribution.

The men all looked at Brenner but they did so subtly, under hooded eyes and with peripheral vision. A quick scan told Brenner that they were all trouble.

Of indeterminate middle age, beards, long hair. Unwashed. Some in dungarees, some in t-shirt and jeans. All openly carried hunting knives on their belts. All had tattoos. None of them were huge, five ten to maybe six foot, but they had the builds of men who worked manually for a living. Fishing, alligator hunting, wood chopping. Forged by the outdoors and annealed by a life of getting by.

Hard men.

Brenner had no reason to start trouble so, instead of just asking for information he ordered a drink.

'You got whisky?'

The bar man stopped polishing for a second, looked at Brenner and then carried on as if he wasn't there.

Brenner tried again. 'How about a shot of Wild Turkey?'

Again the barman ignored him.

Brenner heard four chairs scraping back as the men at the table stood up. He didn't turn around, waiting for them to make the first move.

'Are you him?' Asked one of the men.

'How the fuck should I know?' Replied Brenner. 'I have no idea who you think, *him* is.'

There was a slight pause while the man figured out the answer, then he spoke again. 'The Wolfman. The *Rougarou*.'

'Do I look like a Wolfman?'

Again a pause.

'Jesus,' snapped Brenner. 'What are you guys, like stupid or just slow? Do I look like a Wolfman?'

'*Pic kee toi*,' cussed the man. 'You got a big mouth.'

Brenner turned to face them. Then he smiled. 'All the better to eat you with,' he said.

And he exploded out of his clothes as he morphed into his Wolfman mode.

To be fair, the men were fast. They were looking for trouble and it had arrived in spades. They were hard men, and they were protecting what was theirs. And men who fight on the home front are always better soldiers. Keener, more aggressive. More willing to fight to the end.

As Brenner turned, the barman smashed a full bottle of whisky against the back of his head. 'Don't got no Wild Turkey, asshole,' he shouted. 'You'll have to settle for Old Crow.'

Brenner didn't even bother to turn around. Until the barman had armed himself with a lot more than a bottle of cheap Bourbon, he was no threat at all. But the four men at the table had all drawn weapons, Bowie knives, thick bladed, razor sharp and well-worn with use. Even for a Wolfman, an eight inch blade in the gut had a way of really fucking up your day.

Brenner sprang at the men, growling and snapping his jaws as he did. The men all attacked at once, splitting up and taking him from four different directions, a ploy that was perfect for fighting against a single human being. But not so prefect when fighting a seven foot monster with the reaction times of a snake and the strength of a grizzly bear. But Brenner wasn't looking to kill. He wanted to negate the enemy and then to question them. All that he needed to know was how to get to the island. They were simply in the way and, as such, needed to be removed.

Keeping his claws back he used his clenched fists to incapacitate. Within seconds the four men lay on the floor. Limbs had been broken, but they were alive. Two of them barely so but it was difficult to judge every punch to debilitate but not kill. One of them had managed to cut Brenner's right shoulder. The cut was shallow but long. It didn't bother the Wolfman as he knew that his accelerated healing would knit the flesh within minutes.

Before he could question any of the men on the floor, he sensed someone behind him and spun around just in time to dodge a massive blow from the barman who had upgraded his bottle of Bourbon to a wooden baseball bat with a length of razor-wire wrapped around it, *ala* Negan from the Walking Dead TV series. Brenner grabbed his wrist as the bat flew past, twisting and shattering the bones and tearing the flesh as he did so. Then he grabbed the bat and smacked the barman in the side of the head so hard that it literally exploded.

At the same time the two other men at the bar started firing at him. Both had 1911 Colt 45's. Fortunately, because Brenner was already moving as he fought the barman, none of the initial rounds struck home.

He picked up the table that the men had been sitting at and flung it like a giant Frisbee, spinning it into the two gunmen. Wood splintered and teeth shattered as the two of them were picked up and driven into the wall. Brenner immediately picked up the most *compos mentis* man off the floor and held him at face height.

'I'm looking for Beauchamp,' he growled at the man.

The man spat at him.

'That's not nice,' said Brenner. 'If you don't talk then I'll simply find someone in this town who does.'

The man laughed. 'No one will talk to you. Anyway, you'll never make it out of this town alive.'

'You think?'

'I know.'

Brenner reared back and head butted the man on the bridge of his nose, splintering his cheekbones and splitting his skull. Dropping him back onto the floor, he head for the doorway. But before he could exit, at least ten people with carbines started to shoot at him. The door and surrounds turned into a hail of flying wood splinters as over a hundred rounds of .30 carbine chewed into them. Brenner leapt backwards and sideways to get out of the line of fire.

After a few seconds the gunfire stopped.

Then a man shouted out. 'We have you surrounded. If you come out we kill you quick. Merciful. If you stay in there, we will burn you to the ground. You die in pain. You have two choices, animal man.'

'Where's Beauchamp?' Shouted Brenner. 'Him and I have things to talk about. Go call him and then we can take this whole thing further.'

'Two choices,' repeated the man outside. 'I'm going to count to ten.'

'Are you sure that you can?' Asked Brenner. 'That's a lot of numbers. Maybe, just to be sure, you count to three, but real slow. That should do it.'

'Fuck you,' returned the man.

Brenner took a quick look around the bar. It was wood, no stud wall. Simple, inch thick overlapping planks, chinked with mud and string. He checked that his backpack was still tight, raised up on the balls of his feet and sprinted at the back wall, dropping his shoulder as he hit. There were three men waiting behind the back of the bar and the look on their faces was almost comical when the seven foot monster came exploding through the wall.

One of them simply dropped his carbine and fell to the floor, covering his head with his hands and keening in a high pitched wail. The other two started to react but Brenner was on them, tearing the M1 out of one of their hands and using it as a club to dispatch all three of them.

Then he sprinted down the back road, aiming to break left and come out further down the high street in a flanking movement. But he hadn't gone more than a hundred yards when he felt the burn of a bullet crease across his shoulder. Dropping and rolling into the shadows, Brenner did a quick reassessment of the situation. This was obviously more than a simple lynch mob. There were men out the front of the bar, and obviously more people scattered around the town waiting to catch a glimpse of him and take a few pot shots.

In other words, it was a killing ground specifically set up to kill one person. Him.

For a moment, Brenner contemplated simply

jumping into the bayou and swimming around until he found the island with the shack on it. That way he would avoid having to fight a town full of armed people who all wanted a wolf skin rug. But he knew that the bayou was vast. A myriad of dead-end channels and shifting vegetation. Not to mention that it was infested with crocodiles and alligators and a raft of deadly venomous snakes.

Remembering an old military maxim, leave no enemy behind you as they will rise again to fly at your throat, Brenner scaled the wall of an adjacent house and then swung down from the roof, crashing through the window of the room that the person had been sniping at him from. He grabbed the man by the throat and tossed him through the window, sending him sailing across the street and smashing into the building opposite. Man down.

Brenner leapt through the broken window and back onto the street, heading right. Still intent on flanking the main crowd.

CHAPTER 38

Papa Bruno, who had no idea that Brenner had already left the building, lit the rag on the top of the Molotov cocktail, waited for it to start burning evenly and threw it into the bar. It exploded with a soft thump. Immediately another three followed and within seconds the wooden building was covered in flames. He wasn't worried about burning down the town bar as he knew that Beauchamp would reimburse them.

'Time's up, asswipe,' he yelled.

'I agree,' growled Brenner from behind the crowd of would-be assassins and pyromaniacs.

As they turned the Wolfman charged. He picked up the nearest protagonist by his ankle and, using him as a living bludgeon, laid into the other ten men. Bone crunched and carbines rang out. Brenner felt the burning shock as rounds impacted, gouging into the flesh on his chest and shoulders.

The leg that he was holding tore loose and Brenner dropped to all fours, rolling and snapping at people as he moved.

In the back of his mind he knew that he needed to

keep at least one person alive in order to question them. But the blood lust had taken over. The need to kill was stronger than the need to procure information and the Wolfman savaged and tore all that came within range. Two men tried to make a break for it but Brenner grabbed them both and smashed them together, crushing their bones like bundles of twigs.

Finally Papa Bruno was the only one left standing. He was bleeding profusely from a deep gash above his eye and his left arm hung limply by his side, the elbow broken so badly that the bones stuck out through the skin. In his right hand he held a Colt 45. It was pointed at Brenner.

The Wolfman glanced at the weapon and shook his head. 'You're out,' he growled.

Papa Bruno looked down to see the slide racked back. He dropped the useless weapon and took a deep breath. 'Well that's me fucked,' he admitted.

Brenner nodded. 'Tell me where the island is and I'll let you live.'

Papa chuckled. 'Fuck you, *Rougarou*. You've killed my entire family, what have I got to live for?'

'If you don't tell me, I'll burn this town to the ground,' answered Brenner. 'Then I will kill every last person here. Women, children. Everyone.'

Papa shook his head. 'No you won't. You're a knight in shining armor. You seek justice, not murder. So, with all due respect, fuck you very much.' Then Papa drew a Bowie knife from his belt and ran at the Wolfman.

Reluctantly, Brenner backhanded the man with his claws, opening his throat and driving him to the floor where he twitched a couple of times and then lay still.

The bar burned like a funeral pyre, the flames dancing high into the humid night air, casting flickering shadows of orange and black. Deadly shadow puppets.

Brenner lent down and picked up an unlit Molotov. Then he walked over to the flaming bar and lit the wick. He turned to face the buildings lining the main street.

'Listen to me,' he roared, his Wolfman voice both savage and primal. 'I need to know how to get to Beauchamp's island. Until someone tells me how, I am going to burn this place to the ground. You are all complicit; you all work for this man. You have accepted his silver and in turn you have accepted his corrupt moral code.'

He threw the flaming Molotov through the window of a house opposite. Seconds later the front door banged open, and a couple ran out. Behind them the flames caught the drapes and, soon the building was burning. But before Brenner could question them, they had sprinted down the street and into the night.

Brenner picked up another Molotov. As he lit it, a door two houses down opened and an old lady walked out. She was holding a double barrel shot gun, and it was pointed straight at Brenner's head. He didn't feel threatened as he was confident that he could cover the twenty yards before she could pull the trigger. However, he also knew that there was no way that he was going to attack an old lady. So he plucked the burning rag from the bottle, dropped it and stood still, both hands up. 'What the fuck are you?' Asked the old woman. 'You some kinda werewolf?'

'Some kind of,' agreed Brenner.

'Well what gives you the right to come here and destroy our town?'

'I came here to speak to Beauchamp,' answered Brenner. 'You attacked me. All I wanted was the answer to a couple of simple questions.'

'Beauchamp not here,' snapped the old lady.

'I know. I need to know where his island is, that's all.'

'If I tell you then you'll stop fucking up my town?'

Brenner nodded.

'Follow me,' said the old lady.

Brenner followed her down the main street and to the pier.

She walked to the bait shop and then pointed. 'You see those three channels?'

The Wolfman nodded.

'Take the right channel. You follow it to the end then it breaks into a fork. Go right. Keep going and it leads to the island. Simple.'

'If you lying to me,' rumbled Brenner. 'I'll come back here and kill you.'

'If you get lost, then it's due to your own stupidity,' snapped the old lady. 'Ain't no way that you can kill me then, because if you can't follow such simple instructions then all it means is that you is thick as two short planks.'

'True,' agreed Brenner. 'Are there any boats here? Punts, canoes, air boats?'

'No. Beauchamp ain't dumb. He make sure there no boats here. You wanna get there, you gotta swim.'

'Okay,' said Brenner. He started to walk to the edge of the pier but, just before he did, his hand whipped out and he snatched the shotgun from the old ladies hands and threw it into the bayou. 'Just in case,' he said. 'Would hate to get shot in the back.'

She glared at him and Brenner could tell by her expression that he had been spot on with his assumption. There was no doubt in his mind that the moment he had gotten into the water she would have unloaded two barrels of buckshot into him. And that would have been a major inconvenience to say the least.

Without another look he leapt into the water and started swimming, a slow, steady overhand crawl.

CHAPTER 39

'And then the son of a bitch threw my shotgun in the bayou,' said the old lady. 'But that don't mean nothing because Beauchamp is gonna kill him for sure. That be if he even makes it to the island. Son of a bitch is swimming through the bayou at night so I don't rate his chances.'

There was a general murmur of agreement amongst the group of around twenty people that were gathered opposite the smoldering bar. They were mainly of the older persuasion plus some young couples and some children. A few were armed, but they were obviously not the guns working for Beauchamp, they were the survivors.

It had been almost two hours since Brenner had left and the fires had spread, burning down three houses as well as the bar, before a hastily formed bucket chain had doused the flames.

And now they milled about, leaderless and afraid, but relieved that the monster had gone and that they had survived.

'Well come on then,' said the old lady. 'I reckon that we should collect the bodies and put them in the cold room at the bait shop, or maybe the old barn.'

The group nodded agreement, happy that someone was taking charge, because even bad direction is better than no direction at all.

But before they could start collecting the bodies, a dark, late model limousine pulled into the town, drove up to them and stopped. The driver got out, opened the back door and stood waiting.

Out stepped a man dressed in black. He wore a hat. His pale skin glowed orange in the few flickering flames that still stuttered away in the smoldering buildings. And his eyes looked like two pissholes in the snow. Small, dark and featureless. Dead.

He glanced about and then he laughed out loud. Genuine amusement. 'Brenner,' he said. 'Once again he opens a can with a chainsaw.' He beckoned to the old lady. 'You,' he commanded. 'Come here, old crone.'

'My name is, Ida,' she said.

'Don't care. Quickly now.'

Ida walked over to the stranger and waited for him to speak.

'So, crone,' said Solomon. 'You appear to be the leader of this motley crew of swamp-dwellers, pray tell, when did Brenner leave and where did he go?'

'I already told you,' snapped Ida. 'My name is Ida. Also, I have no idea who Brenner is.'

Solomon nodded. 'True, I suppose that you don't.

He's big. Needs a full body shave. Claws, teeth. Ring any bells?'

'The Wolfman,' stated Ida.

'That's him,' confirmed Solomon. 'Where is he?'

Ida pointed out into the bayou.

'I need you to be a little more specific,' said Solomon.

'Why?' Asked Ida. 'Who are you? What are you going to do?'

'You don't need to know,' answered Solomon. 'Now talk or I shall become vexed.'

The unmistakable sound of a shotgun being racked cut through the night. 'Tell you what, city boy,' said one of the members of the crowd. 'We all a bit sick of strangers coming here and making demands, now it be plain that you ain't no Wolfman so why don't you get back in your fancy foreign car and fuck off. Before we all get vexed at you.'

There was a chorus of agreement added to the metallic sounds of bolts being cocked, shotguns racked and safeties disengaged. The remaining townsfolk felt that they had a potential battle on their hands that they could win, thereby helping to cleanse the bitter taste of failure from their palates. A way of regaining some modicum of pride. So, at the end of the day, they could inform Beauchamp that they had done their bit.

Solomon pursed his lips and then shook his head. 'This is very disappointing,' he said. 'Quite frankly, I don't really have time for this. However, I can see that your minds are made up.'

'Damn right they are,' said Ida. 'So on your way.'

There was a blur of movement and a plume of blood sprayed high into the air above the man who had instigated the disobedience. Before his body had even struck the ground, Solomon was standing back in front of Ida.

All eyes turned to the body that lay twitching on the floor, throat ripped out, blood pooling around it.

'Son of a bitch killed Joachim,' yelled one of the men as he brought his shotgun up to his shoulder and fired.

His shot was immediately followed by a stutter of small arms fire as everyone in the crowd opened up on Solomon.

None of the shots came close as Solomon had begun moving before the first shot had even been brought to bear. But, unfortunately, a full load of double aught had struck Ida in the back of the head and plastered the contents of her cranium all over the sidewalk.

As the gun smoke dissipated, someone called out. 'God dammit, who shot missus Ida?'

'It was, Benjamin,' accused one of the women. 'I saw him do it.'

Before Benjamin could defend himself, there was another blur of movement and shadow and the wet sound of flesh been cut. Two more bodies fell to the floor and, once again, Solomon appeared in the front of the crowd, his expression calm. Patient. A preacher observing his flock.

He glanced down at Ida and shook his head. 'Now that was both unseemly and uncalled for,' he said. 'Killing that nice old lady. You should all be ashamed of yourselves.' He sighed. 'Oh well, tell you what; let's put an end to all of this unpleasantness. You show me how to get to the island and I'll leave you good folk to tend to your dead in a fitting manner. How's that sound?'

One of the men pointed out into the bayou. 'You take that channel. Keep following it right. Can't miss the place.'

'Fine,' said Solomon. 'Where are the boats?'

'Don't got none,' he said. 'They all at Beauchamp's. You gotta swim.'

Solomon turned to his driver. 'Howard, come here.'

Howard walked swiftly over.

'Shoot two of these people,' said Solomon. 'I'm struggling to get them to sense the seriousness of the situation, although, God knows, I have tried.'

'Which two?' Asked the driver.

'How the fuck should I know?' Snapped Solomon. 'Pick two, shoot them, do it now.'

Howard nodded, drew his pistol and fired in one smooth motion. Two shots rang out and a young couple fell to the floor. Both had been shot in the forehead.

Solomon burst out laughing. 'Howard, you dog,' he said. 'You shot the young loving couple. How could you? Man, that's harsh.'

Howard said nothing but his expression betrayed

his anger.

Solomon patted the driver's shoulder. 'No need to get all pissy,' he said. 'Good choice. Well done.' He turned to face the shocked crowd. 'Right, now before we are forced to kill more of you good folk, I need a boat, a nice boat that will get us to the island. You got it?'

The man who had given directions, who by this stage felt that he was starting to live on borrowed time, stepped forward. 'Mister Johnson, he got an airboat. Keep it downriver a mite. Not far.'

Solomon smiled. 'Good. And where is mister Johnson?'

Benjamin pointed at the first man that Solomon had killed.

'Fine,' said Solomon. 'So I suppose that takes him out of the equation. Tell you what, you go and get the air boat. I shall wait here. The rest of you, sit down, don't move and don't talk.'

The man nodded and set off, knowing that instant obedience was the best way to stay being not dead.

And far away, in the very direction of the island, the muted sounds of gunfire punctuated the night air.

CHAPTER 40

Brenner swam fast but smooth. He made no noise and the only sign of his passage was a small expanding wake behind him. He was undetectable by normal human eyes.

Unfortunately, the men looking for him were not normal humans. They were men who had been brought up on the bayou. Men who had hunted Gators since they were children. Men who would take a flat-bottomed skiff, a few lengths of rope and a bolt action rifle and come back the next morning with a boatload of adult alligator carcasses.

In short, when it came to the bayou, these men were the ultimate hunters.

They tagged him without warning. The searchlight bloomed in the night air and lit Brenner up with its white electric light. At the same time the Bren gun opened up. Short, sharp, accurate bursts that plowed up the water around the Wolfman, turning the swamp into a churning maelstrom of death.

Brenner flipped over and dove but as he did so, he felt the burning scour of two slugs. One ripped down his back and the other creased his forehead. The cost of being less than hyper-vigilant.

He stayed under the water and kicked hard, heading for the shadows and vegetation on the side of the channel. Despite his Wolfman enhanced eyesight he could hardly see. The water was murky, and the moon hung low in the cloudy sky.

He came up short against an object that he could only hope was a sunken tree-trunk. He didn't need to be ramming into alligators at this exact moment in time. Thrusting his hand out, he felt the bark and a few odd branches. Satisfied, he swam under the log and came up the other side, nose and eyes above the water. Keeping still as he watched his attackers search for him.

They were making a thorough job of it, playing the white light amongst the reeds and trees and, if they saw anything that looked remotely suspicious, they would open up with both rifle and machine gun. The searchlight quartered its way towards Brenner, working in a grid search pattern. It was only a matter of time before they found him. Less than a minute.

Brenner sank slowly below the surface and pulled the Wolfman-gun from his rucksack. He wasn't worried about it not firing due to its immersion in the swamp as the ammo was watertight and the rest of the weapon had very few working parts. Simplicity at its best.

He pulled back one of the hammers and laid his claw across the corresponding trigger. Then, drifting more than swimming, he let the slight underwater current bring him closer to the airboat.

Brenner knew that he only had one shot at this so he had decided to heed the advice that Colonel William Prescott's gave his troops in the Battle of Bunker Hill back in the revolutionary war of 1775. Hopelessly outnumbered by the British and running low on ammunition, Prescott had told his men, don't shoot until you see the whites of their eyes.

So the Wolfman drifted ever closer. They spotted him when he was but twenty yards away. The searchlight spun, and the Bren opened up but, at the same time, Brenner powered out of the water up to his waist, drew a bead on the boat and pulled the trigger.

The recoil punched the Wolfman back in a perfect half somersault, picking him out of the water and belly-flopping him back down some ten feet away. A massive muzzle flash lit up the night and the airboat simply ceased to exist.

One hundred and twenty balls of double aught rounds tore the life from the three men on the boat. More of the rounds ripped open the large gas tank and sparked off the metal framework. The resulting explosion was more than impressive, and the rolling fireball that ballooned into the night sky was visible from many miles away.

Wolfman, one.

Beauchamp's navy, zero.

From a little over a mile away, Emile watched the

ball of fire as it bloomed in the sky. Then he turned to Mama, a questioning look on his face.

She shook her head. 'He still coming,' she said.

Emile raised an eyebrow and lit a cigarette with calm, rock steady fingers. The night was still young.

***

Brenner drifted through the murky midnight waters, eyes constantly checking for another airboat.

He actually heard the next boat before he saw it. The faintest sound of an oar in an oarlock. The scrape of wood on steel. He kept dead still, only his eyes moving. And suddenly the shape coalesced out of the dark. A flat bottomed fishing punt. Two men inside. Both armed. One holding a handheld battery powered searchlight. They were literally only yards away, hidden in some overhanging brush.

The Wolfman drifted up until he was only two feet from the boat then, using his massive strength, he burst out of the water, grabbed one head in each paw, smashed them together and dragged them into the water, holding the unconscious bodies down until they had ceased to breathe.

Wolfman, two.

Beauchamp's navy, zero.

Brenner carried on moving slowly and steadily in the direction of the island. He saw the bulk of the land at the same time that he saw the second airboat. The pilot had covered the boat with brush and it was almost undetectable but for the faintest glimmer of moonlight off the massive propeller. A tiny sliver of silver on the edge of the blade.

The occupants were looking vigilant, quartering their surrounds, not talking. Pictures of concentration. Brenner knew that he would need to keep this altercation short and sweet. Throwing caution to the wind he dropped below the surface, cocked the hammer back and swam underwater around the back of the boat.

He wasn't aiming for a classic gun battle. He wasn't planning to take prisoners or to give mercy. He was there to clear the path in the most efficient way possible. Keeping lower in the water this time, having learned how vicious the recoil from the Wolfman-gun was, he raised the weapon, drew a bead on the back of the boat and pulled the trigger.

The effect was even more spectacular than the time before. Because the men on this boat had manufactured themselves some homemade IED's. They were nothing fancy. Simple pipe bombs made with Ammonium Nitrate fertilizer and diesel with a touch paper activated detonator and packed with ball bearings. Basically, large hand grenades.

They had seven of them.

The ensuing explosion sent a crushing compression pulse through the bayou and dead fish bubbled up all around Brenner. He rolled onto his back and floated for a while, his eyesight little more than flashes of orange and red, his hearing a high pitched whine and his body in cramp from the compression of the explosion.

One of the ball bearings had struck his left forearm and gone straight through, leaving a clean but very painful hole. At least it had missed the bone and Brenner knew that it would be almost fully healed within the hour.

Wolfman, three.

Beauchamp's navy, zero.

But he had been lucky, and he knew it.

Again, Mama Acadia looked at Emile and shook her head. 'He still comes,' she said. 'But we are hurting him.'

Beauchamp grinned. 'Good. Let him bleed a little; wear away at his arrogance so that we can teach him the meaning of humiliation when he gets here. We can show him that you just do not fuck with Emile Beauchamp.'

CHAPTER 41

Brenner cursed himself for not finding out how many boats Beauchamp had on the bayou. He had taken out three, but for all that he knew there could be another ten. Or even twenty. And to attack the island with so many of the enemy still at his back would be suicide. He had to neutralize them, and he had to do so quickly for he had no real wish to attack a fortified position in broad daylight.

He headed for the shadows, swimming as fast as he dared, searching for another boat as he did so. This time he smelled it long before he saw it. The pungent reek of rotting fish heads, guts and blood permeated the water. It didn't take Brenner long to work out what they were doing.

Chumming the bayou. Filling it with enough odorous fish flesh to attract every gator within ten miles.

'Clever,' he said to himself as he zeroed in on the boat. It was another flat bottom punt, two armed men. One standing watch with an M1 carbine and the other shoveling reeking lumps of fish over the side.

The splashing of the chum covered the sound of Brenner's approach and he simply swam up to the boat and then launched himself out of the river and into the skiff, grabbing the gunman as he did so and snapping his heck before depositing him into the water.

Before the chum deliverer could react, the Wolfman had him by the throat and held him up at face height so that he could look directly into his eyes.

The man swung his bucket at Brenner. It hit him on the shoulder and spilled its contents out all down his front.

Brenner sneered. 'Gross,' he said. 'You know how hard it is to get that shit out of my fur? I'm gonna reek like a dockside whore in the fishing season.'

The man started to choke as Brenner's hold on his neck began to seriously starve him of oxygen.

'Right then,' said Brenner. 'Before you die from asphyxiation, how many other boats are there out here? And let's not do the whole, I'm not going to tell you thing, or I swear, I will tear your arms off.'

Brenner loosened his grip slightly.

'Four skiffs and two airboats,' gasped the man.

'You sure?' Asked Brenner. 'One hundred percent?'

The man tried to nod but couldn't move his head. 'Yes,' he croaked. 'That's all.'

'Thanks,' said Brenner. And then, with a shrug of his shoulders, he broke the man's neck. He dropped him onto the bottom of the boat and got back into the stinking water, heading once again for the island.

As he swam he sensed, on the very periphery of his vision, other beings in the water. Large beings. Over fourteen feet long and approaching a thousand pounds. Perfect killing machines, unchanged by evolution for over eight million years. Scores of them.

Swimming in the bayou alongside the Wolfman.

Brenner decided that he would leave the remaining two skiffs. He reckoned that the time spent searching for them in gator infested waters outweighed the risk of leaving them at his back. After all, it was only four men, a drop in the ocean compared to the army that he was going to encounter on the island.

And not for the first time the Wolfman wondered whether he had made the cardinal error of biting off more than he could chew.

Then the island was there. A lump of land that rose out of the swamp. He could make out a jetty. Moored to it a huge air boat. The largest that he had ever seen. A string of lights lit up a pathway from the jetty up to the residence. A sprawling bungalow on stilts with a small triple story clock tower in the middle. Like someone had taken a fisherman's shack and then replicated it a hundred times, adding larger windows, fancy doors and a higher pitched roof. It looked odd. Essentially incorrect. A homeless man's version of what a rich man would live in. It had obviously been designed to pay homage to the bayou vernacular, but instead it looked as though the builder was being sarcastic. Offering a cutting jibe where there should have been a warm tribute.

Brenner kept swimming, heading for the back of the house, hoping to come ashore on a less well lit part of the island.

And in one of the rooms in the shack, Mama turned to Emile and nodded. 'He here,' she whispered. 'And the gators, they be following him.'

'Will they attack him?' Asked Beauchamp.

Mama shook her head. 'Not yet. Although a gator got a brain that ain't much bigger than a cocktail olive, what little they got is busy telling them to keep away from the Wolfman. They don't know much, but they do know death when it stares them in the face.'

'So what now?' Asked Emile. 'I thought that your big plan was to use the swamp to overcome him.'

Mama scowled. 'Don't be getting snippy with me, boy,' she snapped. 'Just you remember whom you talking to. I say that they won't be attacking him yet. I didn't say that they wouldn't ever attack him. I just gotta commune with them a little. Cloud their thinking. Overcome their fear. Make them think that the Wolfman be a good snack. Now you shut it and let Mama do her thing.'

Beauchamp grinned. 'Sorry, Mama,' he apologized. 'Been an awful long day.'

Mama smiled back. 'Leave me now,' she said. 'I needs to commune with my Loa.'

Beauchamp left the room and headed for the wrap around verandah to check on the security.

Earlier on he had issued most of the men with small two-way radios and he used his now to check that everyone was in position. Satisfied that he had done all that he could, he lit another cigarette and waited.

***

Brenner walked out of the bayou and onto the island. Water streamed off his fur, and the moonlight glinted off his canines as he opened his mouth and sniffed the air. But he could pick up little scent as the stench of the fish chum overwhelmed all else.

Mama Acadia snapped out of her trance and focused her powers. And the water bubbled and frothed as over thirty alligators left the bayou and clambered up the bank, heading for Brenner.

At the same time, Beauchamp's radio crackled into life. 'Boss,' whispered Donatien, one of his Emile's men. 'He's here. Big motherfucker. Looks like the gators are lining up to take bites outta him.'

'Keep me informed, Donatien.' returned Beauchamp.

The Wolfman sensed the gators coming, and he ran away from the water before turning to face them, picking out at least twenty to thirty. He remembered reading somewhere that a bunch of alligators was referred to as a Congregation. Brenner shook his head. If there were ever a less apt collective noun. They should be called a murder. Or a shithouse-full. A congregation brought to mind a line of people asking the vicar to come for tea and cucumber sandwiches. Not a forty sets of razor sharp teeth, and skin that could shrug of a gunshot.

'Maybe they should be called a Senate,' mumbled Brenner to himself as he pulled the Wolfman-gun from his rucksack and thumbed back both of the remaining hammers.

The congregation didn't run. They merely walked at speed towards him. Implacable. Like a forest fire. Unstoppable. He waited until they were only twenty yards away and then he lifted the weapon, ready to fire. As he did so the reptiles broke into a sprint.

People tend to think of alligators as large, slow lumbering animals. Fast in the water and tank-like on land. The average fit human being can be expected to run at a speed of around ten miles an hour. An Olympic sprinter almost twice that. However, an alligator can travel at speeds of over twenty five miles an hour. This means that over a short distance, of say thirty feet, a gator is capable of outrunning a horse.

Their sudden turn of speed took Brenner by surprise and he barely had time to fire before they were on him. But fire he did, moving the barrel fast from left to right. Painting the congregation with two hundred and forty balls of over-charged double aught shot. The effect on the tight packed reptiles was spectacular.

The storm of lead shot killed six of them outright and most of the rest were injured in some fashion. Almost as one, most of them turned and bolted, heading back to the sanctuary of the bayou. However, two kept coming. The first latched onto Brenner's left leg, and the other snapped at him and missed.

The Wolfman grabbed the one on his leg and, using brute strength, he prized its jaws open, pulling until he literally ripped the gator in two. Then he attacked the second one, jumping onto its back and slashing at its head with his razor sharp claws. His talons tore through the thick hide and, after five or six hits, exposed the brain and dealt a death blow.

He had dispatched them both with relative ease but when he stood up, he could feel that the toothholes in his leg would be doing him no favors at all. He knew that the wounds would heal quickly, but those, combined with the numerous gunshots that he had received earlier, were already starting to slow him down.

Mama sank to her knees and grunted in pain. 'He has dispatched them,' she gasped in disbelief. 'There is nothing more that I can do.'

Beauchamp's radio crackled again. 'Boss. He took out the gators. Looks like he's carrying some sort of artillery piece with him. Biggest fucking hand gun I ever did see.'

'Kill him,' instructed Beauchamp. 'Hit him with everything that you have. I'll send the rest of the boys around that side of the island to help.'

'Sure thing, boss.' Donatien turned to his group of six men. 'Right, boss says to kill that fucker, right now.'

The men squinted into the dark, their carbines raised to their shoulders as they searched for the Wolfman. But he was no longer there. A massive, seven foot, four hundred pound creature had simply disappeared in the blink of an eye. He had become one with the darkness.

And then the darkness came to life behind them.

Brenner attacked using his preferred method. Speed and aggression coupled with overwhelming violence. He grabbed the man at the back of the group by his foot and then swung him overhand, smashing him into the others like a human sized medieval flail. Bones broke, shots were fired and lives were ended.

Beauchamp pressed the transmit button on his radio. 'Donatien,' he called. 'Did you get him?'

There was no answer, so he called again. 'Donatien. Come in.'

Finally the radio hissed into life again and a savage, inhuman voice said.

'I am sorry but no one can take your call at this time on account of they're all dead. However, if you'd like to take a number, the Wolfman will be with you as soon as he can.'

'Brenner?'

'One and the same. Start counting the seconds, Beauchamp. Because your life is about to come to an abrupt end.'

The radio went dead.

'Son of a bitch,' screamed Emile. Then he thumbed the open channel on the radio. 'I want everybody up at the shack now. Run. And if you see that fucker on the way here, shoot him.'

CHAPTER 42

Five of them ran along the shoreline towards the shack. Delphine led the way. She was a large girl, as tall as most men as well as being more muscular. She owned her own airboat and hunted gators both legally, during the season, and illegally for the rest of the year.

Next to her ran her dog, Bisou, a cross between a Rottweiler and a German Shepherd. Bisou was scared of no one or nothing. He had even taken on a full-grown gator one season and his missing left eye was testament to the fact that he had stood toe-to-toe with the huge reptile until he had chased it away, ignoring his dire injury.

'Come on, boys,' she urged the rest of the group. 'Mister Beauchamp wants us there toot sweet, so let's keep moving.' She snapped her fingers at Bisou who had slowed down. But then the dog came to a complete standstill. Stopping so abruptly that he actually slid forward a few feet on his haunches. Then, without warning or sound, he simply turned tail and fled, running as fast as he could.

'What the fuck?' Shouted Delphine. 'Come back,

Bisou.'

'Let him be,' growled a voice in the darkness. 'I would hate to have to kill him.'

The group stopped running and crowded together, carbines raised as they stared into the surrounding darkness.

'Where are you?' Asked Delphine. 'Show yourself, coward.'

'If you insist,' replied the voice.

And then he was there.

'Split up,' shouted Delphine. The group obeyed instantly, each man running in a different direction before Brenner could grab anyone. He spun around, seeking to engage but they all started shooting at the same time. Carbines barked and slugs whistled through the air, nipping at Brenner's flesh.

Finally Brenner got hold of one of the men and threw him into the others with a savage fury. Then he rolled hard, lashing out with his talons as he did so, cutting into exposed calves and thighs, slicing flesh and breaking bone.

But these men were well disciplined. They had all hunted with Delphine before and, as such, they were used to working together. They didn't crowd each other or over commit. And when they fired their weapons, they did so with deliberation as opposed to panic. However, it was only a matter of time before Delphine was the only one left.

She stood tall, facing the Wolfman with fear, but controlled fear.

Brenner looked at her with respect. 'Leave,' he growled.

She shook her head and lifted her carbine.

Brenner grabbed the weapon, twisted it out of her grip, curled his claw into a fist and then, almost tenderly, punched her in the face. He heard her nose break, and she fell to the floor, unconscious. He bent down and put her into the recovery position, hoping that he hadn't struck her too hard.

As he stood up, he heard a dull thump and a white illumination flare stuttered up into the night sky, exploding at its zenith as it deployed its parachute and came floating slowly down, bathing the area in blue-white light. Another three followed immediately, and the entire surrounds was lit up like a photo shoot.

Then the shooting started in earnest.

All about him the air was torn asunder by the crack and whip of metal jacketed slugs. Brenner dropped and rolled as the earth all around him was churned up by the massive amount of fire. He glanced around in an effort to pick up where it was all coming from and saw straight away that he had been surrounded.

The two boats that he had not neutralized had anchored close to shore and the four occupants were peppering him with their carbines. Two separate groups of ten plus people in each had flanked him and were laying down enfilading fire. And, finally, a skirmish line of another twenty people were advancing from the shack, laying down sheets of fire as they advanced.

Brenner cursed his arrogance. Beauchamp had played him like a fucking violin, drawing him into the strike zone and then lighting up the area and releasing the bulk of his troops to finish him off.

'Well played, Emile,' grunted Brenner to himself. 'Although if I hadn't been such an overconfident asshole, it wouldn't have worked.'

He dropped to the ground and moved into the shadows cast by the undulations in the soil, using his affinity to the night to cut down on his visibility. He had no real idea on what to do next. The problem with being a werewolf is that, although it gives you the ultimate advantage in hand-to-hand combat, it sucks when it comes to ranged combat.

After a few moments of contemplation Brenner decided that the only avenue left open to him was a Charge-of-the-light-brigade type attack. Balls to the wall and full steam ahead and damn the torpedoes. The only problem with the plan was that he was, most likely, going to be shot to shit.

More and more shots hammered into the ground around him. And then one struck him in the back. Another plowed into his left leg.

'Right,' he said to himself. 'Time to get moving before I die right here.'

And then the shooting stopped. The silence was deafening, leaving his ears ringing.

The sound of a bullhorn screeched out followed by the enhanced voice of Emile Beauchamp. 'Looks like things didn't work out quite like you expected, dog boy.'

Brenner said nothing.

'Tell you what, dog,' continued Beauchamp. 'You stand up, hold your hands… err… paws, whatever, above your head and I'll think about what to do next. Maybe you live, for a while. Maybe you die. I am going to count to ten.'

Brenner tensed his muscles and readied himself for his final charge. If he was going down, then he would make damn sure that he took down as many of these fuckers as possible before he went.

CHAPTER 43

Betty saw a dark blue town car pull up outside the diner. Three girls got out at the same time, almost as if their movements had been choreographed. One of them was carrying a briefcase. They walked towards the diner, entered and stood for a moment.

'Hey, Genevieve,' greeted Boisy. 'You want a cheeseburger and a double thick chocolate shake like usual?'

Genevieve smiled. 'Make that three, Boisy.'

Betty ran up and threw her arms around the girl. 'I didn't recognize you,' she squealed. 'I can't believe it. You're here.'

The two hugged for a while and then Genevieve pulled back. 'These are my friends, Evangeline and Sophie.'

Betty hugged them both, and they all sat down. Within minutes, Boisy served up the cheeseburgers and shakes.

'So,' said Betty. 'Brenner?'

The three girls nodded.

'Did you send him?' Asked Genevieve.

Betty shrugged. 'I don't think that anyone sends Brenner anywhere. I told him that they had taken you and he took it from there.'

'How did you meet him?'

Betty chuckled. 'He came to town to get a tank of gas and ended up destroying Polk's and Goins' drug operation. Then he exacted vengeance on that asshole, Smelly, because he found out that he had molested me. After that he burned down the sheriff's office, the fire station and the mayor's house. Oh, and about thirty plus meth labs. Then he told us to take control of our own lives and start living instead of just surviving. And he left to get you. Where is he now?'

'As far as I know, he went to the bayou to track down Beauchamp. You see, he pitched up at the house, tore things apart, killed anyone who got in his way and told me to go home. But Beauchamp escaped and went to a place that he has in the bayou. Brenner followed him.' Genevieve picked up the brief case, laid it on the table and opened it. 'He also told me to take this.'

It was packed with one hundred dollar bills.

'I reckon there's a little more than half a million dollars here. Brenner said that it's ours because Beauchamp would have no further use for it, on account of being dead.'

Betty stared open mouthed at the cash. At her current rate of earnings it would take her a little over twenty five years to accumulate that much money. And that was only if she saved every cent that she generated and managed to somehow live for free.

Boisy came and sat down at the table with them. He glanced at the briefcase. 'Five hundred and forty six thousand two hundred dollars,' he said.

'What?' Asked Genevieve.

'Five hundred and forty six thousand two hundred dollars,' repeated the cook. 'That how much is inna case.'

'He's right,' said Sophie. 'I counted it on the way here. Exactly right. How the hell?'

Boisy shrugged.

'So what now?' Asked Betty.

'We're free,' answered Genevieve. 'But freedom is hard. Scary. We sort of figured that we would come here see what happened next.'

'We could do with some help,' said Betty. 'This town needs a new sheriff's department, a mayor, some sort of town council. It's only a matter of time until the meth cooks are going to start causing trouble, although Brenner did put the fear of god into them, so that may be a moot point.'

'Betty for mayor,' said Boisy.

Betty laughed. 'Sure, Boisy,' she said.

'Why not?' Asked Genevieve. 'This town is populated by sheep but there are also some good people here. You know everyone, they respect you. You could do it.'

'What about the diner?'

'The girls and I could take care of the diner,' said Genevieve. 'Boisy does all the cooking and I'm sure that we could handle the rest.'

Boisy nodded. 'Betty for mayor,' he repeated.

The four of them sat for a while, finishing their burgers and shakes. Finally Genevieve spoke. 'What is Brenner?' She asked.

'Boisy knows,' said Boisy.

'Oh? What?' Asked Betty.

'Brenner is sad.'

'That's not really what I meant,' said Genevieve. 'But, what do you mean, he's sad?'

'Mister Brenner is sad because he hurts people. He doesn't want to hurt people. Mister Brenner thinks that he is a bad man. He wants to be a good man. But you see, mister Brenner will always be sad because he thinks that angels are shining white and have halos and carry silver harps. He doesn't know that some angels are dark and scary and they carry a flaming sword. Because God needs those types of angels as well.'

Betty smiled. 'I see.'

'So, Boisy,' said Genevieve with a slight smile. 'Are you telling me that Brenner is an angel?'

Boisy nodded, his face deadly serious. 'Of course,' he said. 'Why do you ask? Couldn't you see his wings?'

CHAPTER 44

Before Brenner could move a sound rang out through the still of the night. A gurgled cry and then a wet smack followed by a dull thump.

The odd set of sounds was immediately followed by a chorus of cussing and shouting.

'What the fuck was that?'

'Where's Jacques?'

A similar set of noises rang out but this time it was preceded by a scream of terror.

Then carbines barked and shotguns discharged as the men in Beauchamp's group opened fire on something. Brenner risked a quick glance and saw straight away that no one knew what they were shooting at. Shots were flying in every different direction from left and right to straight up into the air and down at their own feet.

He saw a blur of movement and another body fell, its decapitated head spinning up into the night sky like the devils fireworks.

'Shit,' said Brenner to himself. 'As if I weren't in enough trouble already.' He raised his head again and shouted out. 'Solomon. That you?'

A disembodied voice that seemed to come from all directions at once answered. 'At your service, good man.'

Brenner shook his head and, not for the first time, tried to remember when the psychotic nightcrawler had adopted this faux upper-class way of speaking. Brenner knew that Solomon was born and bred in the Bronx, New York and, if he let it slip, his accent was as thick as molasses in winter.

However, when it came to personality flaws that particular foible didn't even register on the scale. Sergeant Solomon Hopewell was a proper, dyed-in-the-wool army man and worshiped the flag and apple pie above all else. Unfortunately his moral compass was so skewed that there were no longer lines between dark and light. Everything was a subtle shade of filthy gray when it came to Solomon's way of thinking.

And as for his sidekick, Howard, many people saw him as nothing more than an appendage to the master. But Brenner knew better. Howard was a quiet, driven man who followed orders no matter how grotesque or amoral they might be. And that sort of obedience is often even more dangerous than a man like Solomon.

Brenner scanned around him, searching for a sign of Howard. It didn't take him long to spot him, courtesy of his enhanced vision. The driver was perched high up in a Cypress tree, he was holding a G28 compact sniper rifle with night sights and he was zeroing in on the men in the boats.

Brenner waited for Howard to take a shot and then he moved, sprinting towards the right-hand group of ten people that had flanked him. The men in the boats went down like tin targets in a county fair shooting gallery, such was Howard's skill.

Then the Wolfman was amongst his foe once again, bringing his advantage in close combat to full effect. But he was starting to tire and, although his movements were still preternaturally fast, they were microseconds slower than they had been earlier on that evening. And in mortal combat, microseconds make the difference between being a casualty or being a victor.

By the time that Brenner had dispatched the group he had been shot another three times and his healing process had slowed to the point that his fur was now sodden with blood.

The second group had shifted around and were now closer to the bayou, coming at him from a different angle. He took a deep breath and prepared for another onslaught. But as he started running towards them, he heard the methodical cracking of Howard's G28 and by the time Brenner was in amongst them, Howard had already dispatched seven of the ten.

Brenner tore through the remaining three without further injury and then he collapsed on the ground as waves of utter exhaustion washed over him. Slowly he dragged himself down to the waterline and splashed water on his face in an attempt to clear his head.

The parachute flares had all guttered out by now and the night was truly dark again, lit only by the half moon that hung in the cloudless sky.

The gunfire had stopped and when Brenner stood up and looked back towards the house, he could see that the area was strewn with headless bodies. Decapitation was Solomon's preferred method of extermination and he had gone through Beauchamp's best like a combine harvester through wheat.

Only Beauchamp and Mama Acadia were still standing, and they were walking backwards towards Brenner, keeping their eyes on the blood soaked apparition that approached them.

Solomon looked at Brenner and smiled, his teeth and fangs white against his blood painted face. 'Wolfman,' he greeted. 'So good to see you. I must say, I was a little disappointed at how you handled this whole affair. Too little planning and too much bull-in-a-china-shop for my liking. But then subtlety was never your strong suite.'

'What are you doing here, Solomon?' Asked Brenner.

'Come to take you home, old chap,' answered Solomon. 'The boss yearns for your company. Time to join the Bloodborn Project once again. Country before self and all that.'

'Fuck you,' said Brenner. 'You'll have to subdue me first and even you don't stand more than an even chance of doing that.'

Solomon laughed. 'Well why don't we shift the

odds a little then?'

Brenner felt the strike of the bullet before he heard the shot. The 7.62mm full metal jacket round smashed into his right leg just above the knee. The slug missed the bone but transferred enough kinetic energy to the flesh to knock Brenner to the ground like he was the victim of a hit-and-run accident.

'Stay down,' commanded Solomon. 'If you move, then Howard will shoot you again. Understand?'

'Yeah, I understand,' grunted Brenner. 'It's not exactly rocket science, you asshole.'

Solomon smiled. 'Good.' Then he turned to Beauchamp. 'So,' he said. 'Pray do tell, why has Brenner got such a hard on for you?'

Beauchamp shrugged. 'He's insane,' he answered. 'Some sort of personal vendetta.'

Solomon frowned. 'I very much doubt that,' he said. 'You see, you may very well be correct in assuming that Brenner is insane, however, he is a paragon of virtue. He lives his life according to an iron code. Now, I suspect that the basis of that code is not entirely his own. In fact I am sure that he took it from something that he once read. But, be that as it may, it is an honorable code, and he sticks to it. It goes something like - *Never abuse a woman, nor hurt a child. Do not lie, cheat or steal. These things are for lesser men. Protect the weak against the evil strong. And never allow thoughts of gain to lead you into the pursuit of evil.*' Solomon pursed his lips. 'Yes, I think that is it. So, I can only assume that you have transgressed it. And by his reaction I would say that you have transgressed it by a country mile.'

'He's a drug dealer,' said Brenner. 'And he steals lives. Young girls. Forcing them into prostitution. He lies and he cheats. He is evil, and he dresses his evil in fancy clothes and shiny accoutrements. He corrupts and destroys.'

Solomon nodded sagely. 'Fine, case closed,' he said. Then he gestured to Howard and pointed at Beauchamp.

Beauchamp threw his hands up. 'Wait,' he shouted. 'I have money. Power. Influence. There must be some sort of trade that we can make.'

Solomon shook his head and winked. 'Sorry, old boy, but the gavel has come down, and the sentence passed. Cheerio now.'

The shot entered Emile's left temple and exited via the back of his head, taking with it the contents of his skull. He was dead before he hit the ground. Mama dropped to her knees next to him, tears pouring silently from her eyes as she cradled the ruined remains of his head.

'There you go, chap,' said Solomon. 'It's all over. Now we can go home. Get up, time is wasting and you know that I don't want to be caught outside after sunrise.'

'What about her?' Asked Brenner of Mama Acadia.

Solomon shrugged. 'Spent force, old boy. You can kill her if you want. No skin off my nose.'

Brenner shook his head as he stood up. 'No. let's go.'

Solomon waved to Howard. 'Bring the boat around to the dock. It's time.'

Howard slung his rifle, clambered down the tree and headed for the boat that they had stashed in the bushes close to the dock.

Brenner started walking and Solomon followed.

CHAPTER 45

The average lifespan of an alligator is between thirty and fifty years. One Eye Jake was almost sixty. He was sixteen feet long and weighed in at one thousand two hundred pounds.

Over a ton of prehistoric killing machine.

Jake was a legend in the bayou and families had been hunting him for over fifty years with no success other than taking his right eye out with a handgun back in the nineteen seventies.

And when the rest of the congregation had turned and fled from Brenner's artillery piece, Jake had laid low and waited. Watched. Millions of years of evolution primed to ready him for a kill. Patience and persistence.

He was also the most territorial gator in the area and there was no way that he was going to let this strange animal muscle in on his territory.

This is where One Eye Jake lived and woe betide any creature that trespassed on his domain.

With hooded eyes he watched the two people approach the water. As they came level to him he exploded into motion, leaping forward and striking hard. There was the sound of splintering bone as over three thousand pounds per square inch bit down, clamping shut and trapping his prey.

Then he turned and sprinted for the bayou, disappearing under the dark waters with a mere swirl and a thin streak of bubbles.

'Well there's something that you don't see every day,' commented Brenner as he took the opportunity to jump into the bayou and swim underwater until he was far enough away to surface in a concealed manner.

He turned and looked back to see Howard frantically running up and down the shoreline looking for his boss.

Still kneeling next to Beauchamp's dead body was Mama. She hadn't reacted and her eyes stared into middle distance, unblinking and unmoving.

Brenner started to swim, slowly, leaving no sign of his passing.

It was over.

Time to move on.

***

The sun rose. It meant nothing to Mama. She had died during the small hours. She had simply given up the will to live and her spirit had taken flight.

So, although her eyes were open she saw nothing. Not the sunrise. Not Howard as he sat next to the dock and waited.

And not the man called Solomon as he swam to the surface and headed for the deep shadows under the dock. Keeping out of the sunlight.

Solomon looked up at Howard and shook his head. 'Fucking alligators,' he said as he spat a chunk of meat from his mouth.

CHAPTER 46

There are certain bars that seem to exist merely as meeting points for long-haired men with leather jackets, torn jeans and huge amounts of facial hair. These bars are usually situated on the outskirts of small towns, normally on the periphery of the light manufacturing area or warehousing district.

Heralded with a buzzing neon sign, built with the same proportions as a large shoebox and sporting six or seven thundering, clunking air-conditioning units poking from the side windows, it serves cheap liquor and bad food delivered with a staff attitude that simply shouts, fuck you.

As seemed to always be the case, three men were brawling next to the pool table. Standing next to them, screaming at the top of her voice, was the short, buxom over made up, source of the fight. She yelled encouragement and insults with equal verve, spurring the battle on as she did so.

In the far corner, shrouded in both dark and relative silence, sat two old men.

Both were dark-skinned with long gray hair and blue eyes. Bushy gray beards, semi-formal clothing. Open necked white shirts, dark suits, patent leather shoes. The clothes were neat and clean and so threadbare that you could almost pick out the individual strands of the weave.

They appeared to be drinking a white spirit that they had brought in themselves. A practice that was strictly forbidden in the bar. But no one stopped them. No one even looked at them. In fact, it was debatable whether they were even there.

'So, mister Bolin,' said the one. 'You think that he is the one?'

'Yes, mister Reeve, I believe that he has the potential to be.'

'But he is rash. He charges in without thought.'

'Keen,' countered mister Bolin. 'Youthful enthusiasm. No need to mark him down for it.'

'He is violent,' argued mister Reeve. 'Dealing in death comes too easy to him.'

Mister Bolin nodded. 'He is a soldier. He has to fight the good fight and, in doing so, he will need to be comfortable with death. After all, we both know that the only way to truly expunge evil is to destroy it.'

'What about the others that hunt him? There are unnecessary complications. Added difficulties that we don't need.'

Mister Bolin shrugged. 'No one said that it was going to be easy. After all, we are searching for the one, not the many.'

Mister Reeve nodded. 'I agree. So, we shall continue watching?'

'Yes,' confirmed mister Bolin. 'He shows promise. We shall continue to observe.'

He poured another drink, and they both toasted each other.

CHAPTER 47

It had been over a week since Brenner had left the bayou. He had headed vaguely south, towards Texas, cruising slowly, taking in the scenery. Stopping early and sleeping late. Recovering.

But now it was a little under twenty-four hours until the full moon, so he was heading for less populated parts. Looking for a place that he could chain himself up for the first night of the full moon. To stop him hurting innocent people during the change.

He had just stopped for gas and a soda when his satellite phone rang. He grabbed it from his saddlebag and hit the receive button.

'Griff,' he greeted. 'Waasuuup?'

'Listen, Brenner,' answered Griff. 'I don't have much time. I have swallowed a tracking device. It should transmit for the next twenty-four hours or so. My coordinates will show up on your phone. Shit, they're here,' he whispered. 'Look, I gotta go. Help me Brenner, please. You need to come as soon as, before they kill me. Before they kill us all.'

There was the sound of breaking glass. Then a

gunshot.

Then, silence.

Brenner had twenty-four hours to find Griff.

And it was almost exactly twenty-four hours until the full moon.

Shit!

He checked the coordinates on his phone, jumped onto his Harley, gunned the engine and took off.

****

Thanks for taking the time to read the first in 'The Bloodborn Project'. I was looking to create a character that brought to mind the high plains drifters of old. A western hero that rode into town on a dark horse, delivered justice and retribution in equal measure and then rode off into the sunset.

A modern day gunslinger with a dark secret.

I hope that I did the premise justice.

If you liked the book (or, even if you didn't) I would really appreciate it if you took some of your precious time to leave a review. Just a few words and a star rating. These reviews are an author's life's blood and we rely on you to provide us struggling writers with the transfusion!

If you did enjoy the book, then please try the next in the series – "**Wolf Spirit**".

Thanks again – and if you would like to get in touch with me to give me some feedback, advice or even to simply say hi, my personal email is zuffs@sky.com. I will always answer.

BOOKS IN THIS SERIES

Project Bloodborn
Every month he shifts into a killing machine. Can this former soldier save an innocent town and send evil packing?

Vietnam veteran Ded Brenner detests his savage nature. On the run after the US government brutally turned him into a werewolf, he rides America's highways desperately seeking a cure. But he wastes no time when he discovers a terrified community forced to work under a drug kingpin's iron fist, and transforms to deliver a brutal punishment.

Tearing through the criminal scourge, Brenner claws his way into the belly of corruption. But when his past finally hunts him down, it's more than just the full moon that could cost this black-ops beast his humanity.

Will the vigilante shifter survive the fight for freedom?

WOLF MAN is the thrilling first tale in the Project Bloodborn urban fantasy series. But there are more books…many mare!

Book 1 - Wolf Man
Book 2 – Wolf Spirit
Book 3 – Wolf Killer
Book 4 – Wolf Warrior
Book 5 – Wolf Pack
Book 6 – Wolf King
Book 7 – Wolf Guardian
Book 8 – Wolf Soldier
Book 9 – Wolf Shield

Here is a short excerpt from Book 2 – Wolf Spirit. Take a look and see what you think…

PROLOGUE

It had been over a week since Brenner had left the bayou. He had headed vaguely south, toward Texas, cruising slowly, taking in the scenery. Stopping early and sleeping late. Recovering.
But now it was a little under twenty-four hours until the full moon, so he was heading for less populated parts. Looking for a place he could chain himself up for the first night of the full moon. To stop him hurting innocent people during the change.

He had just stopped for gas and a soda when his satellite phone rang. He grabbed it from his saddlebag and hit the receive button.

'Griff,' he greeted. 'Waasuuup?'

'Listen, Brenner,' answered Griff. 'I don't have much time. I have swallowed a tracking device. It should transmit for the next twenty-four hours or so. My coordinates will show up on your phone. Shit, they're here,' he whispered. 'Look, I gotta go. Help me Brenner, please. You need to come as soon as, before they kill me.'

There was the sound of breaking glass. Then a gunshot.

Then, silence.

Brenner had twenty-four hours to find Griff.

And it was almost exactly twenty-four hours until the full moon.

Shit!

He checked the coordinates on his phone, jumped onto his Harley, gunned the engine, and took off.

1

The room was dark. Not pitch black. There was just enough light for Griff to make out the approximate size of the place as well as the fact there were at least another ten people there with him.

Like him they appeared to be shackled to the floor. A length of steel chain ran from a cuff on his right wrist, through a U-bolt in the floor to a corresponding cuff on his left wrist. There was enough play for him to sit or lay, but not to stand.

Griff had no idea how long he had been there. He remembered them coming for him. The phone call to Brenner. The fight. Them trashing his Winnebago. Tearing the hard drives from his computers, picking up his laptop, grabbing all the paperwork they could find.

He smiled to himself. Amateurs. They would find nothing on the hard drives. He had followed the protocol of the ultra-paranoid hacker and hit the red button as soon as they had shown up. Not only had that scrubbed the drives clean but it had also implanted a virus of his own making onto them, thereby ensuring anyone who tried to read them would suffer the consequences. Using the "I Love You" virus and blending it with the "Code Red" virus, Griff had written a new virus he called the "Dear John". As soon as they attempted to open his hard drives the "Dear John" would penetrate their systems and start to reproduce itself at an exponential rate until it had eaten up all the systems resources. Finally, it would display a message that read. "I'm so sorry, John. It's not you, it's me".

Griff was under no illusions the virus would result in the end of things. Quite the contrary. He knew, as soon as they had been attacked, they would come and find him and attempt to get info from him the old-fashioned way.

But that was later. He could hear the people around him moaning. Some coughed, some whimpered. A few, like him, remained silent. He could smell urine. So he could deduce they had been chained up long enough for people to start to lose control of their bladders. But it still didn't give him much of a time frame.

He knew he had been knocked unconscious during the take down but it had only been for a short time. Then they had drugged him. He had felt the needle in his arm, he had fought unsuccessfully against the soporific feeling, then he had woken here, in chains. With a hangover rivaling the very worst he had ever had before.

A door opened and flooded the room with light. People gasped and a few let out desultory shouts. Cries for attention, demands for explanations. They were ignored as three men walked straight toward Griff. They hauled the old man to his feet, unlocked his shackles, and dragged him from the room, closing and locking the door behind him.

The sun blasted his eyes as he exited. Mountains in the distance. Scrubland. Almost desert. Fences. Clapboard bungalows laid out in rows like some sort of military camp. Or prison. Griff stumbled and they pulled his chains tight, slapping him on the back of the head as they did so.

They crossed what seemed like a parade ground then through a doorway into one of the basic buildings. Along a corridor and into a bare room with three chairs and a wooden table.

There they slammed him into one of the chairs, pulled the chain behind his back and shackled him.

The restraints were tight enough to prevent him from moving.

Sitting on the edge of the table was a man Griff immediately picked out as a leader. The three men who had dragged him in showed obvious signs of deference to the leader in both their body language and attitude.

He was short, slightly overweight, and wore a charcoal suit, red necktie, and black brogues. Shiny pink face. A large square cut diamond sparkled on his pinky finger, bringing attention to his soft manicured hands. But his eyes were his most arresting feature. Deep brown with ovoid pupils, they protruded slightly from their sockets. Almost as if he had just been choked. And the whites of his eyes showed all around the iris, giving him a fervent maniacal demeanor.

The eyes of a prophet.

He stared at Griff for a while. Silent. His eyes boring into his very soul. Then he spoke.

'They call me, The Pastor,' he said. 'And you would be, Reece Griffin. Sergeant. Army Ranger, Vietnam. Two silver stars, four purple hearts.' He stood and approached Griff, hands behind his back. He stopped two steps away and nodded. 'Thank you for your service.'

'Yeah,' said Griff. 'And fuck you very much, Pastor. What the hell am I doing here?'

The Pastor raised an eyebrow then made a small gesture with his head. A barely discernable tilt. One of the men who had dragged Griff in, walked over and punched the old veteran in the nose. Griff heard it break. A sound akin to a boot stepping on gravel. He felt the blood flow, warm and sticky, into his moustache and beard. He could taste the iron flavor in the back of his throat.

'You see, Mister Griffin,' continued the man in the suit. 'We know who you were, now we just need to know who you are at this moment in time. Are you simply some washed up Vietnam vet with PTSD or are you working for someone? And, if you are on someone's payroll, who?'

The man stood and waited in silence for a while. Eventually Griff spoke. 'I'm sorry, was that a question?'

The man nodded. 'Who do you work for? Why were you looking into our business? How much do you know?'

Griff thought for a few seconds. What he didn't want to tell the man was the truth. He didn't work for anyone. He was looking into their business due to a random search while looking for something else and it had led to them. And, finally, he knew next to nothing about them aside from the fact that only hours after he had started to look into them, people had tracked him down and kidnapped him. The reason Griff was loath to divulge this info was because he knew as long as they suspected he worked for some outside agency and they thought he knew more than he did, then they would have to keep him alive to get the information out of him.

The moment they knew he was an ignorant old man who worked alone and knew nothing ... well, then he would have definitely outlived his usefulness and could look forward to little else than a shallow grave in the middle of nowhere. A fate he would like to avoid if at all possible.

Of course, there was a downside. He knew they would start putting some serious pressure on him to get the info out of him. And that meant his broken nose was the least of his worries. Worse was to come, of that he was certain.

However, he also knew Brenner was coming. So it was only a matter of time. And no matter how hard these boys thought they were, Griff didn't sweat them. He had been captured by the VC once while in Cambodia and had suffered in one of their camps for six weeks before he had escaped. These boys were rank amateurs and he knew he could take anything they threw at him and more.

'So, would you like to talk?' asked The Pastor.

Griff nodded and mumbled an incoherent sentence.

Again The Pastor gestured toward one of the henchmen who stepped forward, putting his face close to Griff's. 'Talk to me,' he said.

Griff repeated himself, mumbling for all he was worth.

The man leaned forward to try to make out what Griff was saying.

And the old veteran whipped his head forward. His forehead smashed into the henchman's nose with a satisfying crunch and Griff yelled out his satisfaction.

'Yeah,' he shouted. 'Take that, you asshole.'

The other man in the room didn't even wait for instructions before he started to beat on Griff, raining blows down on him like he was a piñata.

Just before he blacked out he wondered how long it would take Brenner to find him.

2

Brenner had been in Kentucky when he had gotten the call from Griff. The info on the satellite phone had been linked to the tracker Griff had swallowed and showed the veteran was somewhere in West Texas. Over one thousand miles and at least sixteen hours' drive away.

So Brenner had set off immediately, driving through the night without sleep. Desperate to find his friend before the tracker went off-line. And hopefully, also before the rising of the full moon when he would be forced to turn into an uncontrollable monster for the night.

The sun started to peek over the horizon and Brenner checked his watch. He had been on the road for fourteen hours straight and he was nearing his destination. Unfortunately, Griff's estimated time frame of twenty-four hours had been incorrect. In fact his signal had faded then cut out after only twelve hours.

But Brenner had sufficient info to know his friend

was somewhere near the foothills of the Guadalupe Mountains. So he headed along the interstate, searching for any town near the last known signal. Riding northwest he kept going in the general direction the last signal had registered, using dead reckoning as his navigational aid. The roads changed to single lane and finally to dirt tracks with no signage.

He slowed down, negotiating the potholes and ridges, keeping an eye out for rocks. After a minute or so of riding he saw a car parked next to the road, nestled in a pull-off area. As he got closer he could see it was a sheriff's car. A white Ford Crown Victoria. On the door a single star and the word, Sheriff.

Brenner noted that there were no county markings or motto. Unusual but not unheard of.

As he rode past, the two deputies turned their heads to follow him but didn't otherwise move.

Half an hour of careful riding later, Brenner saw another car. This one a white Ford Explorer. Also, a single star, the word, Sheriff. No county identification, motto, or contact numbers. Again, the deputies watched him go by but didn't give chase or pull him over.

Twenty minutes later Brenner saw a sign. It was professionally done but not the usual Government Issue. "Pepperpot – 15 miles". Reflective white paint on a dark green background.

Minutes later he passed another sign that read, "Welcome to Pepperpot".

The town was bigger than he would have thought. The main road was still dirt, but the sidewalks were cobbled and the buildings looked like a Disney version of a Wild West town. Wood buildings, hand-painted signs, and old-fashioned window displays. Many of the shops had hitching rails for horses. But there were no gun toting cowboys. Instead a smattering of normal looking people went about their day-to-day business.

Brenner rode slowly through the town and was surprised to find the main road simply petered out into a rough dirt track at the edge of the town. So he turned and went back, looking for the local barber shop.

He reckoned the barber usually knew the local gossip. He could get a haircut and use it as an excuse to ask about anything strange that may have happened of late, without having to explain himself as he would if he approached the local law enforcement.

He glanced at his watch as he walked, reminding himself he had to leave with plenty of time before nightfall. He had spotted a few places on the way in where he could stay for the night and chain himself up.

Ready for his inexorable transformation into the monster he became at the beginning of every full moon.

The shop was easy to spot. Outside the classic red and white barbers pole.

Brenner pulled up, parked his bike next to the

hitching rail and walked in.

A man in a white coat sat on one of the two barber chairs reading a newspaper. He was the only person in the room and when Brenner walked in he greeted him with a sigh and a surly look. As if he was offended by the stranger's custom.

'Looking for a trim,' said Brenner.

'Have you made an appointment?' asked the barber.

Brenner looked around the empty shop and raised an eyebrow. 'Seriously?' he asked.

The man in the white coat didn't say anything, he simply stood and waited for Brenner to answer his question.

Brenner took a deep breath. 'No. Actually, I didn't make an appointment. I've just got into town and figured I'd take a chance you were free.'

The man shook his head. 'Sorry. No appointment, no haircut. There are rules, you know.'

'But there's no one here,' argued Brenner. 'Look. Empty.'

'Be that as it may, if your name isn't in the book then you ain't setting your butt down in the chair.'

'Okay,' returned Brenner. 'Could I please make an appointment?'

'Sorry, no,' said the man. 'We're fully booked.'

'You gotta be shitting me,' exclaimed Brenner.

'No need to be all aggressive, sir,' said the barber. 'Rules is rules. Now if you don't mind, right of admission is reserved and I'd like you to leave.'

'Fucking idiot,' mumbled Brenner as he exited,

closing the door behind him and taking a right turn, figuring to walk along the street a bit and see if there was anyone else he could ask a few questions.

Before he had walked ten yards, both of the sheriff's vehicles he had seen earlier pulled into the main street. The Explorer stopped in the middle of the road and the Crown Victoria continued until it was level with him.

He kept walking, eyes ahead but the Crown Victoria edged in front of him and stopped. They had obviously followed Brenner in as he had last seen the car over an hour before.

The two deputies stepped out of the car and approached Brenner. They seemed alert but not especially aggressive. Merely two cops doing their job. Brenner stood still and waited.

'Sir,' said the one deputy. 'Please put your hands on the roof of the vehicle and stand with your legs apart.' He gestured toward the Ford Victoria as he spoke.

'Why?' asked Brenner.

'We have received a complaint that you have been harassing one of the townsfolk. Acting in an aggressive and threatening manner.

Brenner smiled. 'Not true. I asked for a haircut and he refused. Told me I needed an appointment. So I left. Anyway, that was like a minute ago, what did he do, get straight on the phone, and report me for wanting a trim? Man, thank God, I didn't ask for a shave. What then, would I have been accused of murder?'

The deputy's hand moved to his holster. 'Sir, step forward and place your hands on the roof of the vehicle. Do it now.' Brenner sighed, stepped forward, and placed his hands on the car.

The deputy kicked his feet back a bit, making sure Brenner was off balance, forcing him to lean forward, his weight on his arms. He ran his hands over Brenner, frisking him for a weapon. Then he pulled his hands behind his back and ratcheted on a pair of handcuffs.

After that he opened the back door. 'Please get into the vehicle, sir.'

'Really?'

'Yes, sir.'

Brenner complied. He knew this was obviously a misunderstanding and there was no need to antagonize the cops.

Small town deputies were often overzealous in their interpretations of the law. It had happened to Brenner many times before and, he was sure, would happen again in the future.

He would apologize, they would tell him off, maybe issue a warning and he would be on his way. He had to get out of town in the next couple of hours at the latest.

The sheriff's car was clean. Unusually so. Brenner had been in the back of police cars before. Many times. They normally all had the same smell. Cheap cleaner overlaid by ingrained sweat, puke, and the acid tang of fear. This car smelled of cigarette smoke, burgers, and coffee.

Still, he couldn't complain. With his wolf-enhanced sense of smell he was pleasantly surprised not to have his nostrils assailed by the usual putrid odors.

The sheriff's office was at the beginning of the main street and the drive took a little less than thirty seconds. Brenner wondered why they didn't simply walk there.

The deputy stopped the car, exited, and opened the door for Brenner, instructing him to lead the way into the building. The office was like many others Brenner had seen in the last few decades. Clean and tidy. A charge desk. Corridors leading off to the right. An open-plan office behind the desk.

The deputy guided Brenner along the corridor. At the end was a steel-covered door. He opened it and pushed Brenner inside.

Interrogation room. A sturdy wooden table, bolted to the floor, a steel hasp fixed into the tabletop. A single steel seat on the one side. Also bolted down. Opposite, two slightly more comfortable chairs. Freestanding. The standard two-way mirror stretched along the one wall. A bank of overhead fluorescents buzzed slightly, giving off a blue-white light that bleached out all color and made everyone look like they were recovering from a bout of flu.

The deputy pushed Brenner into the seat then he opened the cuffs, pulled Brenner's arms to the front, reattached them, and clipped them to the hasp on the desk.

Then he left the room, pulling the door closed behind him.

Brenner waited, aware of the minutes ticking by. The approach of the night. He hoped they weren't planning on keeping him here for the duration.

Eventually, after an hour of waiting, the door opened and a man walked in. He was dressed in the same uniform as the deputies but he was older and Brenner picked up a sense of leadership about him. It was obviously the sheriff.

He pulled up one of the chairs and sat opposite Brenner. Neither of the men spoke for a while.

'Finally the sheriff nodded. 'My name is Sheriff Harris. You got a name?'

'Brenner. Ded Brenner.'

'What sorta name is, Ded?'

'Name my pappy gave me,' answered Brenner.

The sheriff pulled out a pack of cigarettes. Lit up. He didn't offer. 'So what you gotta say for yourself, Mister Brenner?' asked the sheriff. 'Storming into my town, threatening my people. Cussing and demanding.'

'No, sir,' answered Brenner. 'Simply passing through. Felt the need for a haircut but apparently you have to make an appointment, even if the place is emptier than a banker's heart.'

The sheriff took a long drag on his cigarette before he spoke again. 'You weren't just passing through,' he said. 'There ain't nowhere to pass through here to. This is the end of the road. And according to my deputies you headed here from the highway. Directly here, no detours. So you obviously came here with a purpose. Now I wanna know what that purpose is.'

Brenner thought before he answered. He didn't want to mention Griff in case it started to complicate things and the sheriff decided to keep him there past sundown. So instead he simply said.

'I got lost.'

The sheriff shook his head. 'No. You traveled along a dirt road for over an hour. You didn't take any turnoffs, didn't deviate. And when you got here you headed for the barber. Just the place I would have gone to if I wanted to get the lowdown on the local scuttlebutt. So, I say again, what you doing here, Mister Brenner.'

The sheriff lit another cigarette and waited for a response but Brenner didn't answer.

'Who are you working for?' asked the sheriff. 'FBI, Homeland Security? Private contractor?'

'Sorry, Sheriff Harris,' answered Brenner. 'I honestly have no idea what you're talking about. I'm just a drifter. I'm going from one place to another place. There's no ulterior motive, nothing deep or sinister. Just a man and his bike and the road.'

The sheriff puffed on his cigarette, his eyes fixed on Brenner. A patient man. No one spoke until the sheriff had finished his smoke. Five, maybe six minutes. An eternity of silence.

Then he stood. 'Fine,' he said. 'Maybe a night in the cells will reveal the truth.'

Brenner shook his head. 'No.'

The sheriff laughed. 'You don't get to dictate terms, boy,' he said. 'Either you tell me what I wanna know or you stay here until you do.'

The door opened and two deputies walked in. They had obviously been watching through the two-way mirror and had entered to take Brenner to a cell.

Brenner felt a wave of panic flow over him. He couldn't be here tonight. People would die. They didn't have a cell strong enough to stop the monster. For their sakes he had to get out.

Now.

Summoning his strength, he took a deep breath and jerked his hands apart, shattering the handcuff's chain as he did so. Then he leapt up and headed for the door.

The sheriff jumped in front of him as he moved and Brenner shouldered him aside, trying not to hit him too hard as he did.

As he barreled into the sheriff, he heard the sound of a gas cartridge being fired and he knew someone had fired a taser. Fifty thousand volts arced through him like a tsunami, shutting down his nerve endings, cramping his muscles, and sending his heart into overdrive. With a yell of defiance, Brenner turned and yanked the weapon out of the deputy's hand, bringing the assault to an end.

But at the same time the second deputy fired. Then the sheriff. One hundred thousand volts drove Brenner to his knees, at which stage the deputy whose taser he had removed, stepped over to him and hammered his baton into the back of his neck, smashing the big man to the ground.

The last thing Brenner registered was the taste of blood in his mouth and the overwhelming feeling of despair and guilt at what he knew was going to happen in a few short hours' time.

Well, once again thanks.

Just a final bit of shameless self-promotion!
If you do enjoy my work – please look out for my other series's…

Emily Shadowhunter.

There was a problem… London was full of Vampires.

So, the Foundation sent Emily to kill them - the thing is, they didn't know about her dark side.

On her eighteenth birthday, everything changed for Emily. All she wanted was an iPhone and a pair of designer shoes. Instead she got superpowers and a mission to save the world.

Now she's surrounded by the undead. Werewolves, Shapeshifters, Magicians and Vampires. And she thinks that she just might be in love with one of them.

Not to mention the fact that an ancient evil is slowly taking over her soul.

You'll love this genre-busting adventure, because being bad has never felt so good before.

The Forever Man

His training prepared him for anything. This invasion will test his limits...

American Embassy, London. Master Gunnery Sergeant Nate Hogan stands for integrity. But he's not equipped to face violent solar flares that decimate the population, plunging survivors into war and chaos. Following a strange compulsion to leave his post for Scotland, Hogan discovers massive radiation from the cosmic disaster has transformed him into a superhuman.

But after a savage army of Orcs arrives in the UK through a rift in time and space, he's hopelessly outnumbered by the bloodthirsty horde. With the fate of the world hanging in the balance, he embarks on a desperate quest to alter the course of history.

Can Master Gunny Hogan win a one-man war against a powerful foe and prevent the end of humanity?

Pulse is the 1st novel in the genre-bending Forever Man fantasy series. If you like post-apocalyptic heroes, battles against mythical creatures, and wild temporal jumps, you'll love this crackling mashup.

Dead Declan.

Declan O'Brian has been in Hell for over fifty years...
...and the Angels have just set him free!
Because sometimes you need a bad man to do a good thing.
O'Brian used to be one of the IRA's top hitmen. But after so long in the netherworld he's no longer cutting edge. Can a man who reckons flares and sideburns are high fashion, and thinks that the internet is something you catch fish with, fight an ancient evil in today's settings?
Maybe, if he can ever figure how to turn his cell phone on.
Fortunately for us, he's Irish, he's mean, and he hasn't forgotten how to kick ass.

Wolfman

Every month he shifts into a killing machine. Can this former soldier save an innocent town and send evil packing?
Vietnam veteran Ded Brenner detests his savage nature. On the run after the US government brutally turned him into a werewolf, he rides America's highways desperately seeking a cure. But he wastes no time when he discovers a terrified community forced to work under a drug kingpin's iron fist, and transforms to deliver a brutal punishment.

Tearing through the criminal scourge, Brenner

claws his way into the belly of corruption. But when his past finally hunts him down, it's more than just the full moon that could cost this black-ops beast his humanity.

Will the vigilante shifter survive the fight for freedom?

WOLF MAN is the thrilling first tale in the Project Bloodborn urban fantasy series. If you like supernatural mavericks, dark secrets, and vicious battles, then you'll love Craig Zerf's rollercoaster adventure.

Wolf Spirit

Ded is back - kicking ass and taking names as usual. Griff is in trouble - and this time, Ded might not be able to save him...

Wolf Killer

The adventure continues...

Wolf Warrior

Wolf Pack

Wolf King

Wolf Guardian

Wolf Soldier

Wolf Shield

Printed in Great Britain
by Amazon